SIR WALTER'S LADY

SIR WALTER'S LADY

Judith Saxton

Severn House Large Print
London & New York

This first large print edition published in Great Britain 2003 by
SEVERN HOUSE LARGE PRINT BOOKS LTD of
9-15, High Street, Sutton, Surrey, SM1 1DF.
This title first published in regular print format 2003 by
Severn House Publishers, London and New York.
This first large print edition published in the USA 2003 by
SEVERN HOUSE PUBLISHERS INC., of
595 Madison Avenue, New York, NY 10022

British Library Cataloguing in Publication Data

Saxton, Judith, 1936 -
    Sir Walter's Lady. - Large print ed.
    1.   Throckmorton, Bess, 1565? - 1647 - Fiction
    2.   Raleigh, Sir Walter, 1552? – 1618 - Fiction
    3.   Great Britain - History - Elizabeth I, 1558 – 1603 - Fiction
    4.   Great Britain - History - James I, 1603 – 1625 - Fiction
    5.   Love stories
    6.   Large type books
    I.   Title   II. Turner, Judy, 1936 - . Ralegh's fair Bess
    823.9'14 [F]

    ISBN 0-7278-7309-1

To Brian, with love

Printed and bound in Great Britain by
MPG Books Ltd, Bodmin, Cornwall.

Introduction

This was my first book I wrote and I did so for a bet. I was grumbling about the postal strike in 1971 and my friend Jean suggested that I tried writing a biographical historical novel.

There was a fiver on it and I was missing my small weekly cheques for stories, articles etc, so I had a go and enjoyed the experience immensely, particularly the research.

When I got the letter of acceptance, it was just like the birth of my first baby: a heady and wonderful experience, which I have since repeated sixty odd times (books, not babies)! So my friend certainly started something when she urged me to 'have a go'.

ONE

'WHAT WILL I BE?'

Bess Thorockmorton knelt on the window-seat in her bedchamber, looking out at the pleasant gardens surrounding Beaumanor and the peaceful Leicestershire countryside beyond. The April sunshine fell warmly through the small leaded panes, flushing her creamy skin and making her hair shine like polished satin.

Behind her on the fourposter lay her new gown. The gown that her stepfather, Mr Adrian Stokes, had given her to celebrate her seventeenth birthday. Bess turned from her contemplation of the bright spring day to admire once again her newly acquired finery. Blue as the April sky, blue as her own wide eyes, the gown lay on the rumpled sheets, enticing Bess to put it on and parade downstairs to show herself off like a little peacock to her brothers, the servants – oh, anyone!

Bess hesitated, then turned to the mirror and stood before it, gazing at her reflection. Even in her linen shift the lines of her young body could be seen. The supple waist, the long slim legs, the promise in her rounded breasts.

But Bess ignored her body. She concentrated on her face. So much was happening to change her life! Her brother Arthur was at the Elizabethan court, doing his best to get her a post as maid of honour to the Queen. At seventeen she was on the bright road to womanhood. Surely all this must show in her expression?

But the face she had been looking at every morning for the past year gazed back at her. A wide, humorous mouth, straight nose and determined chin. Eyes bright and curious. Nothing unusual, thought Bess resignedly.

She frowned at her reflection, then leaned forward to examine herself more closely.

What will I be? she wondered. Will I be beautiful? Or will I be like the Queen who makes all men believe her beautiful, even at almost fifty years of age?

By half closing her eyes and gazing at herself through her thick gold lashes, she could make the mirrored girl appear mysterious, different.

'I'll go to Court, and take it by storm. Men will long for me and I'll marry the richest and handsomest of them all,' murmured Bess.

Then her excited imagination took her a step further. She eyed her reflection critically, seeing the bloom of youth and health as an enemy to sophistication. She tilted her chin, pulling a haughty face.

'Why shouldn't I marry and be Queen myself one day? Her Grace hasn't named her successor yet. Why, I share stepfathers with a Queen – the Lady Jane Grey's mother, nasty old thing, married Mr Stokes before my mother did. Perhaps I'll be his second stepdaughter to be crowned.'

A voice spoke from the doorway, making Bess jump and whirl sharply round.

'And what happened to Lady Jane Grey, your majesty? Do you wish to follow in her royal footsteps to the Tower and thence to the block?'

The speaker, a tall young man with fair curls, grinned teasingly at his sister, seeing the colour mount to her cheeks.

'Nicholas!' squeaked Bess. Then, recovering her composure, she added with dignity, 'People who listen at doors are – are—'

'Traitors? Treasonable vagabonds? Scurvy rogues?' put in Nicholas helpfully.

Forgotten was the grace and dignity that were to be hers. Forgotten her heavy weight of years. Bess flew across the room and boxed Nicky's ears whilst he held her at bay as best he could, laughing and tickling her whenever she paused in her onslaught.

'You'll never get to Court, you little hell-cat,' he said cheerfully, pushing her back on to the windowseat.

'Why not? Who are you to say? Arthur will persuade her Grace, you see,' said Bess.

'Persuade?' laughed Nicholas. 'Even if good old Arthur tells the Queen you're an angel of goodness and piety, one sight of you clouting the first person who annoys you, whilst you use language learned from the stable...'

'From my brothers,' muttered Bess, nursing a bruised wrist.

'From the stable,' Nicholas went on inexorably, 'the first sight of you doing that will be enough to make her Grace realise her mistake and send you about your business.'

Bess sniffed scornfully.

'I shall have no cause to lose my temper at Court,' she told the grinning Nicholas. 'My only brother at Court doesn't taunt me like you do.'

Bess lowered her head demurely and brushed an imaginary tear from her lashes. Nicholas, far from being impressed, shouted with laughter.

'Bess, you've seen too many plays,' he declared. 'That's Arthur's fault. You and he are never happier than when you're weeping over a tragedy or laughing at bawdy jests.

But don't put on the airs of a great lady yet, little sister. I know you too well. Wait till you arrive at Court.'

'You said I'd never get to Court,' muttered Bess resentfully. 'Anyway, you shouldn't come into my room when I'm in my shift. It shows a lack of respect. It's not gentlemanly either,' she ended triumphantly, leaning back on the window and scuffling the rushes on the floor with her bare toes.

'When you act the lady, I'll act the gentleman,' promised Nicholas. 'By the same token, when you get to Court I'll show you respect. Not before, little sister.'

'Nicky, am I such a sad romp because I've only brothers?' asked Bess curiously. 'Are other girls sweet and quiet and biddable? Do they guard their tongues? Oh, I wish I had sisters instead of six brothers.'

'I'm not staying here to be insulted,' said Nicholas, not moving nevertheless. 'Besides, since our Uncle Carew adopted me I've spent most of my time at Beddington. Why can't you follow the advice of our mother?'

'She's too busy to give me much advice,' grumbled Bess. 'I *must* get to Court, Nicky, I must! I'll have to pick up Court manners at Court, that's all.'

'You're young yet,' said Nicholas from the height of his nineteen years. 'You'll learn.'

Then, relenting at the pathetic droop of his sister's mouth, 'Why, you're quick and

11

clever, Bess, you get that from our father. When you do get to Court I've no doubt you'll outshine 'em all. But be a good lass and come downstairs now, there's a message come from Arthur and mother wants to speak with you.'

Bess gave an ecstatic squeak and bounced across the room, grabbing at the new gown.

'Nicky, you brute! Why didn't you say so at once? Ooh, a message from Arthur and mother wants me! Perhaps he's got me a place at Court. Perhaps he reminded the Queen of the services our father did for her. Perhaps...'

'Perhaps nothing. The less the Queen has to be reminded that we're Sir Nicholas Throckmorton's offspring the better for all of us, I imagine. Now don't get all excited and hot to hold, Bess, or mother will give you a lecture – well deserved, too, you wanton. Don't start tearing off your shift with me still in the room – I'll send Joan up to help you dress.'

Nicholas left the room hastily, shutting the heavy oak door behind him before his indignant sister could think of a suitable reply.

Waiting impatiently for Joan to come and help her into the awkward underwear that went with such a magnificent gown, Bess thought to herself that she really must learn to guard her tongue. Suppose she had been

12

acting one of her more fanciful parts and it had been Arthur who had heard, or even her mother? She would have been whipped, besides getting yet another lecture.

Seventeen, she decided, was a marriageable age. She must cast off childish things. It was at this inauspicious moment that Bess remembered a favourite game she had played with her brothers. Tumblers. She had been better at it than any of them. But now the boys had outgrown such games and she could no longer display her prowess. Should she try the backbend for the last time, whilst she waited for Joan? It could do no harm to try, she decided.

Bess stood with her legs apart, facing the window, and gradually bent backwards until her fingers touched the floor and her body formed an arch. Pink-faced with the exertion, she was about to slowly raise herself to an upright position again when a horrid realisation overcame her.

She was stuck! The last time she had done the trick she had been an immature fourteen, slim and green-boned. Now, though she could still do the backbend, she couldn't bring herself triumphantly to her feet again.

Scarlet-faced, she was still struggling when Joan providentially came into the room and rescued her young mistress.

'Be thankful 'twasn't Lady Throckmorton that caught you playing such hoyden's tricks,' she scolded as she helped the chastened Bess to dress. Bess stuck out her lower lip but said nothing. What a beginning to her birthday! Then she caught a glimpse of herself in the mirror and cheered up. The stiff formal gown might feel uncomfortable and the unaccustomed wheel for the farthingale might nip her tender waist, but it was worth it. The blue taffeta sparkled in the sunshine and the stiff half-ruff which tickled her neck framed her vivacious little face most becomingly.

Joan draped a *peignoir* round her shoulders and began to coil the girl's long hair into a low chignon. When she finished, Bess sighed with pleasure. She looked so elegant and adult – even the irrepressible Nicholas would be impressed. Turning slowly and carefully, she smiled graciously at Joan and rustled slowly out of the room.

Joan stood in the doorway watching the slim figure glide down the stairs.

'Acting again. I wonder who she's being this time?' she muttered as the golden head disappeared from view. Shaking her head and smiling despite herself, Joan went slowly back into the bedchamber and began to shake out the sheets.

Downstairs, Lady Throckmorton sat before the window, warming herself in the April sunshine as her daughter had done, busy with her thoughts.

14

Left a widow comparatively young, with six sons and a daughter to rear and very little money, she had been glad enough to accept Adrian Stokes when he had offered for her. For his part, she knew, his previous marriage to the Duchess of Suffolk had been a great step up in the world. He had borne with her imperious ways patiently, and at her death she had left him a rich man. So when he decided to marry again, he had been able to choose a woman he really wanted to wed – the still beautiful widow of that famous diplomat, Sir Nicholas Throckmorton.

Mr Stokes and his Duchess had been a childless couple and now Lady Throckmorton knew that her husband's love for herself was almost less than his love for her children. But his favourite was Bess. She was young when her father died – only six – and Lady Throckmorton had married so soon after her first husband's death that the child looked upon Mr Stokes as the only father she could remember.

Lady Throckmorton had kept her name and title, as was fashionable, but she was very fond of her second husband. She brought the children up on tales of their father's deeds and the history of the Throckmorton family, which went back to the fourteenth century. This, she considered, was no more than her duty. But she always made sure that these reminiscences took place when Mr Stokes was absent from the house.

Bess, with her bright, sunny nature treated her stepfather with real affection, though she answered him back and argued with him in a way she would never have dared to do with her mother. But the boys – well, it was more difficult for them. They were older when Lady Throckmorton introduced a new father into their lives. Nicholas, spending so much time at Beddington with Sir Geoffrey Carew, was carelessly fond of Mr Stokes, but the other boys had found it difficult to be respectful, imitating Mr Stokes' Welsh accent and commenting on the temper that went with his red hair.

But now Arthur at least, thought Lady Throckmorton, was away from home, on the road to success. He had inherited his father's good looks but not the late Sir Nicholas' brilliant and impetuous mind. Arthur at Court might cause little stir amongst the hearts of the maidens but he would cause little trouble either, thought his mother thankfully.

Absently caressing the letter that lay on her lap, Lady Throckmorton thought about her only daughter. What *was* to be done with Bess? Her father had left her £500 for a dowry, but the money had been lent to the Earl of Huntingdon and never repaid. Now her only real hope was that Arthur could somehow persuade the Queen to have the girl at Court, as a maid of honour. There she would meet all who were noblest and best in the land and would stand a chance of both earning the Queen's approval or even affection. Eventually she might even attain a brilliant marriage, despite her lack of dower.

With her looks – mused Lady Throckmorton, then caught herself seeing her daughter in her mind's eye. She was a lovely girl to be sure, but she had other qualities – an unaffected natural charm combined with a sweet nature which might prove even more valuable than her beauty.

Here at home, Bess met few young men. Friends of her brothers, some neighbours. But at Court she would mix with the cream of Elizabethan society. Lady Throckmorton conveniently flicked out of her neat memory the other types of men one might meet at Court. The hangers-on, the intriguers, the practised seducers, the royal favourites who could be a maid's undoing.

I can rely upon Bess to act for the best, thought Lady Throckmorton firmly. When all the circumstances were explained her daughter would set herself out to be obliging, she was sure.

The door opening slowly effectively brought Lady Throckmorton out of her daydreams. Bess paced proudly into the room, the blue taffeta whispering round her feet, her richly coloured hair smooth as satin.

'You look well enough, child,' said Lady Throckmorton, but the tears of pride which welled into her eyes gave the lie to the temperate praise.

Bess, smiling, swept a magnificent curtsy, then ran into the room and sat herself carefully beside her mother, her eyes going eloquently from the letter to her mother's face.

Lady Throckmorton laughed.

'Well, well,' she said indulgently, 'Arthur was always in great favour with you. Now he'll be greater.'

'Is it – Court?' questioned Bess, for once almost timid in her eagerness.

'Oh, as to that, I could say yea and nay. Arthur says he has had some few words with the Queen's grace. He has presented her with a pair of scented gloves, made of finest leather and most delicately embroidered. He said,' her eyes twinkled, 'they were embroidered by his little sister.'

For a moment, sharing the open secret that Bess was no needlewoman, mother and daughter looked very alike. Then Lady Throckmorton returned to the perusal of her son's letter.

'Arthur says the Queen does not give lightly and so far she has shown him no particular favour. When he petitions for the post of maid of honour for "his most dear sister" she puts the question from her. But he thinks she will give way. He says you are to be made ready for the Court, my child.'

Bess raised her winged eyebrows enquiringly. Her mother shook her head, smiling indulgently.

'Don't plead ignorance, Bess, you know well what your brother means. You've known too much of the company of lads. You say what enters your head, not what is politic. You have no dignity, no womanly accomplishments, few graces. Why, you cannot dance! All these things must be learned, before the Queen gives her consent.'

'I'll learn, I'll learn,' promised Bess fervently, her eyes alight. 'God's blood, may the day be soon.'

'Don't use stable-talk,' reproved her mother sharply. 'And I say it will be many a year before you can sew a straight seam, let alone possess the womanly graces Arthur would have you display, or the womanly discretion and discreetness that I desire to see in you.'

Bess said earnestly, 'I'll do my best, mother. I'll really try to learn, so that I may do you and Arthur credit.'

Her mother eyed her indulgently. She meant so well, the sweet child!

''Tis your birthday,' she said affectionately. 'We won't spoil today with lessons in Court manners. Just take care of your gown so that Adrian sees it at its best. Tomorrow your lessons will begin.'

She left the room and Bess jumped lightly to her feet, twirling and whirling, the farthingale swaying wildly as she skimmed across the floor.

'My, you're a fine lady now, Bess,' said a deep, slow voice from the doorway.

Bess knew that voice. It was her eldest brother, William. No one ever laughed at or teased William. No one schemed for him or planned a marriage. No one told him what was afoot in the broad world, for William would not understand. Because William Throckmorton, who should have been his father's heir, was simple. Kind and gentle, but so slow-witted that he had to be told when to dress, eat, mount his horse; even when to go to bed.

He stepped into the room and sat down, watching the flight of the vivid creature who danced so gaily with round, wondering eyes.

'I'm going to Court, Will,' sang Bess, rumpling his hair as she darted past him. 'When I'm a great and famous lady I'll not forget you, darling Will.'

'What will you be famous for, our Bess?' asked Will after a lengthy pause. Nick, who had entered the room and was watching the scene with some amusement, answered for her.

'Why, Will, how can you ask?' he said with mock incredulity. 'She'll be famous for her beautiful handwriting and the unexampled brilliance of her spelling. I shouldn't wonder if they make her Queen of the Ciphers on the strength of it.'

Bess sank dizzily down beside Will and stroked the hair she had rumpled, as a mother would fondle her child.

'Yes, my spelling will go down in history, Will,' she laughed.

TWO

COURT AT LAST

Three girls sat round the fire in the small pannelled room, huddled close to the hearth for warmth, their numbed fingers working at their stitchery.

Frances Hastings, small, plump, pretty as a ringdove, widened her bright black eyes.

'What, mending your apricot silk again, Anne?' she asked teasingly. 'Aren't you tired of wearing that gown yet?'

'Aye, heartily,' answered Anne, smiling at the younger girl. 'But we don't all have endless gowns to dazzle the young men's eyes and compete with her Grace. What are *you* doing, Mistress Almighty? Not making that ruff higher?'

'Well, it will be higher,' admitted Frances, smiling fondly at her handiwork. 'I'm adding a rufflet of lawn. When the goffering iron's been on it, I'll be the envy of the Court.'

She turned in her seat and spoke to the

third girl, quieter than her two friends.

'What are you reading, Marjory? You've scarce set a stitch since we sat down.'

'It's only a street ballad about Mary Stuart – very likely false,' she replied in her soft, rather timid voice. 'But have you made up your mind, Frances, whether you want Arthur Throckmorton? I thought the last sonnet he sent you charming.'

'I care no more for him than Anne cares for her apricot silk gown,' answered Frances promptly. 'Like her, I wear him as my conquest until I find a better.'

Her companions giggled and worked on until Anne announced, 'There! Finished! If the Queen goes on a Progress next summer, so shall my much-worn apricot silk. Oh, but the weather's cold, even for November. This is a draughty old room.'

'My feet are icy,' agreed Frances. 'Every draught in Christendom seems to blow up my skirt. I can't even feel the warmth of the fire through this velvet.'

She plucked impatiently at her skirt, then impudently pulled it up, revealing shapely legs clad in woollen stockings, gartered above the knee.

'Frances!' exclaimed Anne and Marjory in shocked voices, Anne adding, 'Suppose one of the young gentlemen were to come in...'

The remark was interrupted by a perfunctory knock on the door, followed by the impetuous entrance of a tall young man, whose narrow shoulders were made to appear wider by the padded sleeves of his doublet and the short, full cloak that he wore.

Frances scrambled to her feet and felt with relief the folds of concealing velvet swish round her ankles. She curtsied, but her eyes were bright with anger.

'Mr Throckmorton! What brings you here in such haste? You startled us,' she demanded in a voice of strong displeasure, ignoring the muffled giggles of her friends.

Arthur flushed, but today even Frances' snub didn't altogether chasten him.

'It's my sister, Bess. She comes to Court to be sworn into the Privy Chamber as maid of honour. The Queen has at last given permission and Bess rides here as soon as maybe. I trust you will grow to know and love her as I do, Mistress Hastings,' he blurted out, reddening under the cold glance of his beloved.

He lingered a moment, then on an impatient exclamation from Frances about the draught he mumbled an excuse, gave a flustered bow, and left the room.

Amongst the three young girls the small pebble of information spread a few ripples and died. Another maid of honour, that was all. The girls discussed the clothes they would wear to grace the Christmas festivities at Greenwich.

24

Back in his own chamber, Arthur combed his hair and thought of the adorable Frances.

Bess was forgotten.

A few days later, Bess found herself threading the narrow London streets on her mare, Susan, whilst her stepfather rode beside her on his great black gelding.

Bess was in a state of nervous excitement, enjoying the sights and sounds, though not the smells, that surrounded her. She was not too self-centred, however, to be unaware that Mr Stokes had a nasty cough not helped by the chill November air. The sound of the horses' hooves rang sharply on the cobbled streets, and steam from their breath mingled with smoke from the fires of the roast chestnut vendors.

Bess glanced uneasily at her stepfather. He was well muffled, but he couldn't hide the sound of his cough even amongst the street cries which rang out so loudly.

'I wish you hadn't insisted on accompanying me, father,' Bess said suddenly. 'I could have managed very well with John from the stables.'

'What, Bess, would you take all my pleasures from me? I'm not in my dotage yet you know,' protested Mr Stokes. 'I shall lodge in London for a few days, seeing the sights. I'll even look up some of my old cronies.'

Bess, riding round a great tip of foul-smelling rubbish, wondered aloud that the pile was not burned up, so that the air might be purer.

'Aye, that lot was ripe for burning,' chuckled her stepfather. 'Put your little nose into your posy, Bess, and sniff the sweets of the late roses. These Londoners wait till the authorities order them to fire their rubbish. After all, they have no use for it to make the soil richer, like we landowners.'

He chuckled again. Whenever Bess boasted that she was the daughter of a famous diplomat he retaliated, with his rumbling laugh, that he was landed gentry, and what might have caused unpleasantness between them had become an old family joke.

A cluster of young men burst forth from one of the tall houses leaning over the street and Mr Stokes said they were apprentices, probably intent on mischief.

'There seem to be more rich folks and more beggars in London than in the country,' Bess remarked presently. 'People seem either very rich and proud, or beggars, shouting their wares in rags.'

Mr Stokes smiled fondly down at her.

'Your eyes are dazzled, my fair one. See – there is an honest housewife, plainly dressed, buying chestnuts for her little girls, to keep their hands warm. Your eye has lighted

26

on what is strange and exciting only. There are good, bad and ordinary in London as there are in the country, or in Leicester.'

Bess bounced in her saddle, making the mare cavort.

'London is marvellous, exciting, the world!' she exclaimed. 'I thought Leicester was *such* a town, but London makes it seem a mere village.'

But Mr Stokes wasn't listening. 'We meet Arthur at the sign of the Black Swan,' he muttered. 'Is this the place, Bess? Your eyes are younger than mine.'

'Yes, and there's Arthur. Look, father, staring at that young woman.' She giggled. 'He hasn't seen us. Let's ride up quietly and surprise him.'

'Nonsense, girl, I'll give him a shout. Hey there, Arthur!'

The hail that brought Arthur running gave Mr Stokes another choking fit, but he swung down from his horse and handed the reins to a waiting stable lad.

'We'll say goodbye here, Bess,' he told his stepdaughter. 'Arthur will take you to be sworn into the Privy Chamber by the Vice-Chamberlain.'

Leavetakings were soon over and Arthur rode beside Bess to Hampton Court to be sworn. Then he left her with some misgivings amongst the other maids of honour. He needn't have worried. Bess was a friendly girl and it didn't take her long to become one of the circle that surrounded Frances Hastings.

Frances had meant to hold Bess at a distance but she enjoyed her company, all the more when Arthur suddenly fell in love with Mistress Darcy, a conceited girl unpopular with the other maids of honour. Frances admitted she was glad and Bess knew why.

'You'll be able to enjoy the celebrations of Accession day on the seventeenth and all the Christmas gaieties without my brother dangling after you,' Bess accused, laughing. 'You'll flirt with such abandon there won't be a heart left whole by the New Year.'

'Frances, Bess, the Chief Gentlewoman of the Privy Chamber has called a meeting of the maids of honour. It's in her chamber. Come now, leave your work till later.'

It was Marjory who spoke and the three girls ran along the corridors of Hampton Court until Mistress Parry's chamber was reached. They went in to find the room already half full of girls. The air was heavy with the scent of pot pourri, for Blanche Parry was blind. The scent, she told her friends, brought back memories of the flowers she would never see again.

'She's old – between seventy and eighty, I suppose, but still much beloved by the Queen,' whispered Frances. 'Her advice is good, too, Bess. You listen closely.'

28

Bess nodded, already a trifle awed by the sight of the upright old lady sitting on her hard chair, her white hair arranged deftly over padding to hide its sparseness. Her eyes seemed to hold wisdom and understanding of them all.

Bess would have been more than a little disillusioned if she had known what Blanche Parry was thinking. Was it any use, thought Blanche, to try to impress on these bright young things the responsibility of their position as maids of honour? Modern religion, modern thought, all led to loose behaviour, she mused darkly.

When the room was full a servant whispered to Mistress Parry and she began speaking.

'I want you all to remember for as long as you live at Court that the Queen must and will regard you as she would her own daughters,' she began. 'To her Grace your honour is her honour. Your disgrace reflects on her. She means you nothing but good and you must not mind that sometimes she grows impatient or a little rough when you displease her, for she has all the cares of this realm on her shoulders, as well as trying to be a mother at Court to all you young things.'

She paused and the girls exchanged speaking glances. So the Queen was a mother to them was she? Most had already had a taste of the Queen's displeasure. She could be charming one minute, playing for them whilst they sang or showing a dance step.

Then someone would make a tactless remark, sing out of tune, or drop an earring the Queen was about to place in her ear. Without warning came the stinging slap, the angry scold. Such punishment must be borne without complaint, for to argue resulted in a pinch from long white fingers and a cry of, 'Get you gone, impudent wench.'

Blanche, unsuspecting, went on, 'So remember, children, you serve a great Queen. Since she was a child she has borne burdens heavier than any you'll ever be called upon to bear. Serve her well and you'll earn her gratitude – perhaps even her love. Serve her ill and you serve yourselves ill, for to be sent from Court in disgrace is no pleasant thing, and the Queen does not relent.'

THREE

DEATH OF A LADY

'So the Queen of Scots is dead at last, the whole of England rejoices – and what do we do? Tremble when the Queen of England speaks for fear someone has once more annoyed her.'

It was Frances who spoke, bitterly but truthfully. Mary Stuart, after years of being a source of constant discontent shut up in her various prisons in England, had been beheaded at last. But the Queen, who had known what it was like to be endangered even by friends when next in succession to the throne, could not join her subjects in their joy.

Elizabethan courts were always on the move, so that whilst they were at Richmond, Hampton Court might be made fresh and pure again for the next royal invasion. But now Elizabeth excelled herself. Restless, plagued by guilt and unhappiness, the Queen moved her household constantly.

Lambeth, Richmond, Windsor, Oatlands, Greenwich – the Queen no sooner moved into a palace than she longed to be away from it.

Bess was now twenty-two. In appearance she hadn't changed much from the innocent young maid who had first ridden to Hampton Court. But now she was no inexperienced wide-eyed girl. She knew her mistress – the pursing of the lips that heralded an outbreak of tears or temper. The treatment meted out to a girl who smiled upon one of the Queen's favourites. The sudden fits of generosity, the displays of real affection.

'It's still springtime,' she said in answer to Frances' despairing accents. 'I'm going into the gardens to see what flowers are in bloom. *They* are not blighted by the winter that seems to have numbed you all.'

With that cutting remark, Bess swept out of the room and along the corridor leading into the pleasant gardens sloping down to the river.

As the cool breeze fanned her hot cheeks, she felt guilty for having flown out at Frances. Poor girl, she had spoken no more than the truth. Now, whilst loyal Englishmen slept at peace in their beds because the menace of Catholicism was removed, for Gloriana, needless guilt fought sleep.

Bess had followed the reports of the trial and felt happier and safer once the irrevocable decision had been made, but she could understand her royal mistress's soul searchings.

What she wants, she was thinking as she strolled quietly indoors again, was something to take her mind off the Queen of Scots. Or someone, perhaps?

Entering the Presence Chamber once more she was unprepared for the animated discussion which met her.

'He's so *handsome!* That golden hair, and his bright, sparkling eyes – I swear I wish he would look at me instead of at her Grace.'

'Robert Devereux, Earl of Essex. What a lovely name! He's young enough to be her son though. Too young for me.'

That was Frances, tactless as always.

Heads turned swiftly as Bess entered the room, and a sigh of relief came from more than one pair of lips.

'Ah, gossiping again, girls?' said Bess sweetly. 'It's a good thing her Majesty has been in a – er – quiet mood, or the Presence Chamber wouldn't be the most discreet spot to pick for exchanging confidences.'

'Oh, Bess, how you scared us,' said one damsel reproachfully. 'But you missed the most gorgeous man – an adonis, truly.'

'The Earl of Essex – I've heard of him,' answered Bess thoughtfully. 'He's the son of Lettice Knollys, the famous beauty. When she married Leicester the Queen, who once loved her cousin most truly, referred to her as "the She-Wolf". Right?'

Frances nodded.

'He's only a lad, though he's so handsome. Rumour has it that Leicester is frightened of being replaced in the Queen's favour by Sir Walter Ralegh, so he's sent his stepson to Court to plead his interest.'

'Ah, her "Eyes" see more than one gives them credit for,' murmured Bess, grinning at Frances.

Neither girl had seen much of the Earl of Leicester, who had sensibly retired to the country when the Queen discovered his illicit marriage. What they had seen hadn't captivated them much. A large man true enough, but running to fat, with his eyes bulging and his hair thinning.

They knew, however, that the Queen was said to have loved her Sweet Robin Dudley, christening him her 'Eyes', for she nicknamed all who were close to her.

'I wonder how Ralegh will enjoy being polite to a glorious lad about fifteen years his junior?' someone said maliciously.

Bess felt a slight flush warm her cheeks. Sir Walter's bold black eyes were apt to linger absently on her trim figure as she went about her duties, just as his handsome person lingered in her dreams. But Bess realised that for a time at least all his thoughts were with the Queen. Through her and only through her could he realise his ambitions, and one had only to glance at him to realise that ambition and pride ruled this dark, mocking man.

'Why should he be polite?' she answered swiftly. 'He's never polite to anyone. If he likes them, he's nice to them, if he doesn't, he's rude. That's why the Queen is so fond of him – and why no one else can bear him.'

'Ah ha, now there you're wrong,' said Marjory, smiling slyly at Bess. 'Let's not pretend he's only favoured by the Queen. He's always hopping about between England, Ireland and the Continent, yet he managed to dishonour two maids of honour – and they loved him well enough to keep quiet about it.'

The girls giggled and Bess said briskly, 'At any rate, it seems likely that between the two of them her Grace will forget her melancholy.'

Frances nodded thoughtfully.

'If I sat between two such men, like a rose between two handsome thorns, I'd forget melancholy existed,' she admitted.

'Who would not?' asked Marjory. 'By the same token, perhaps your admirer will be allowed back to Court, Bess.'

'Which one?' asked Bess, making her friends laugh.

She was popular with the men at Court for her open, friendly manner as well as her golden beauty. Frances, who believed that one's admirers should be made to suffer, frequently scolded her friend for being too kind to men.

'Why, Frances, remember I've six brothers,' Bess would tease. 'I've come to consider men as almost human!'

Frances would pretend to scowl, telling Bess severely that she might as well make men suffer whilst she could, for after marriage it was the woman upon whom all the suffering fell.

But Bess just laughed. Her most ardent admirer at the moment was young Robert Cecil, Lord Burghley's second son. He was no beauty certainly, being short and slight, with a crooked back and a pale, thin face. But he was sensible and intelligent. He could be very good company once he had conquered his unbearable shyness. Bess was fond of him and felt secretly annoyed with the girls when they laughed at poor Robert.

Bess was without vanity. It never occurred to her that Robert Cecil sought her out for her beauty and charm. Surrounded by the prettiest daughters of the noble and wealthy, she thought herself below the average for looks. Most of the girls who had been at Court when she first arrived had married and left. Arthur was gone, living with his in-laws in Colchester. He hadn't married Mistress Darcy, especially since her tale-bearing to the Queen had landed him in Marchelsea prison for two months. Instead he had fallen in love with a young girl scarcely nineteen, Anna Lucas. She was a sweet, gentle girl, and Bess had found no difficulty in loving her as a sister.

Soon, Bess knew, Frances would leave, for she was betrothed. Some of the girls stayed on – she and Marjory were both of noble but impoverished stock so that young men thought twice about courting a woman who would bring nothing but her pride and beauty to the marriage bed.

However, though Robert Cecil obviously admired her and enjoyed her company, he and his father were out of favour for the time at least. The Queen had felt obliged to find a scapegoat to prove she hadn't desired Mary Stuart's life. So she had imprisoned the man who had carried the warrant, and banished the Cecils from Court. They were probably at Burghley House in Hertfordshire, thought Bess, working for their return to the Queen's favour.

'If Essex and Ralegh are with her Grace, do we have to stay here?' enquired Bess.

'Yes indeed. Lady Norris came out a little while back to whisper that the Queen might have need of us later on, as she is seeing the French Ambassador tomorrow and wants to be sure her dress is prepared and ready for the occasion.'

'Why a special attire for the French Ambassador?' asked Bess, then laughed at herself. 'Oh, of course, if Essex is at Court...' She left the sentence unfinished.

'Do *you* admire Essex, Bess?' asked Marjory a few evenings later as the girls prepared for bed. Bess considered.

'He's the vainest man I've ever known. And he's – well, two-faced. He courts the Queen as if she were the fairest damsel in the kingdom, and eyes us as if he's stripping us down to our shifts in his mind. No, I don't think I do like him.'

'A good thing, since the Queen is so taken with him,' said Marjory philosophically. 'But I think he has something to be vain about, nevertheless. I've never even imagined a handsomer man.'

Bess, climbing into her small hard bed, smiled secretly, to herself. She not only imagined a handsomer man, she knew one. A man who had a lean sunburned face and a determined jaw. A man who had thick black hair crisply curling, so that his beard and moustache had a natural upward tilt.

A man, thought Bess ruefully, who never noticed her.

It was hot in the palace of Greenwich this July weather, so the maids of honour had carried their needlework out into a small, secluded garden where they could work and talk and enjoy the breeze from the river.

They were engaged on embroidering tapestry curtains, but their fingers moved slowly and even their lively tongues were quieter than usual.

'Is there any gossip, Bess?' asked a comparative newcomer, Meg Radcliffe, re-threading her needle with scarlet silk and beginning once more on the rosy poppy she was embroidering.

Since Lord Burghley and Robert had been reinstated, Bess was often the recipient of the younger Cecil's confidences. She betrayed nothing that he asked her to keep to herself, but usually managed to pick up snippets of information for her friends' interest.

'Why, very little,' Bess answered, after giving the matter some thought. 'There are all the usual foreign threats of invasion and reprisals for Mary Stuart's death. Robert thinks Spain means business this time and will try to punish her Grace.'

'Only Essex can punish. When he frowns, the sun goes in,' someone chimed in dramatically.

'Essex draws you apart sometimes, Bess,' said Meg impulsively. 'Does he please you? Why do you give him so little encouragement?'

'Because I have the full use of my senses,' answered Bess sharply. 'God's wounds,

Meg, I can't afford to be dismissed from Court because that conceited puppy smiles at me. Neither do I want his attentions. They lead to one end.'

One of the girls turned a dark pink and glanced under her lashes at Bess. Bess laughed.

'Oh, Phillippa, do you listen to the golden words of the golden god and believe them?' she mocked. 'Remember old Blanche – "The Queen never forgets". If Essex meant honourably towards you – which I dare swear he does not – you'd probably ruin his chances of advancement at Court for many months, and you know how long he can sulk!'

Phillippa raised her head and said defiantly, 'I only trifle with him, Bess, as he does with me. He's so *very* handsome and charming, don't you agree?'

'Handsome and young and foolish. When he begs the Queen for some favour she gives it to him. When he begs you to share his bed you'll be too deep in love to give him the no word. He's always been spoilt and got his own way. Don't let him seduce you, you silly child.'

Phillippa gave Bess a venomous look and said under her breath, 'I wonder how long your resistance would last if Essex stormed your citadel,' but Bess only smiled.

She was safe from Essex. It was the other

she would have to guard against. When she heard the Earl's polished drawl her heart did not miss a beat, but when the voice had a deep Devonshire burr, and a touch of mockery, her heart bumped in her breast and delicious prickles ran up and down her spine.

One day Ralegh's bound to notice me, she thought. Then what shall I do? Run to his bed and my ruin? Or be strong-willed, as I advise poor Phillippa?

As luck would have it, he noticed her the very next day. Essex was in the Privy Chamber with the Queen. Ralegh, as Captain of the Guard, stood at the door. In the Presence Chamber young men were playing cards, the maids of honour were reading, writing letters home, stitching at some new piece of finery.

Suddenly they heard Essex raise his voice angrily.

The words 'I have no joy to be near you, when I know my affection so much thrown down, and such a wretch as Ralegh highly esteemed' came clearly to the listening ears.

Instantly, every sound in the Presence Chamber was hushed. No one spoke. Even the card players were like statues, the cards suspended in midair, their mouths at half-cock.

Bess, looking full at Ralegh's face, saw the look of devilment in his dark eyes. As his

41

glance fell on her, the devilment melted into mirth. Their glances held with almost magnetic force as Essex shouted, 'What comfort can I have to give myself over to the service of a Mistress that is in awe of such a man?'

Again the Queen was silent and Essex left the Privy Chamber impetuously, brushing deliberately against Ralegh as he did so.

Ralegh, apparently impervious, was still watching Bess. His gaze lingered on her full red lips for a moment before his eyes rose to hers once more. In that moment, it seemed to Bess, something passed between them. Something more than the shared joke over Essex behaving like a brat not out of the nursery.

Then from behind the door the Queen's voice cried imperiously, 'Ralegh!' Abruptly he turned and entered the Privy Chamber. For a moment the listeners heard the low murmur of voices, then laughter. Shared laughter.

As the heavy door swung shut the Presence Chamber began to buzz with conjecture. Bess alone was silent. She knew, without being told, that sooner or later now, Ralegh would seek her out.

She was right.

The visit of the Ambassador had gone off in grand style. Essex, having flung out of the Privy Chamber the day before, had apparently decided to stay away for a while. So the Queen had greeted the Ambassador with Ralegh beside her, both clad in raiment so glorious that it dazzled the eye.

Only the maids of honour, thought Bess, knew the work that had gone into the arraying of Gloriana. Her face had been carefully painted and powdered to hide the two or three tiny marks left by the smallpox she'd had years before. Her wig, a glorious if improbable shade of red-gold and most marvellously curled, was carefully placed and secured with a pearl and emerald circlet from which flowed an airy veil of finest gauze. Her elaborate Court dress was put on over numberless petticoats, ruff underproppers made of wire were cunningly fastened in place, and then the neckline cut low enough to suggest, but not low enough to reveal, became the resting place of many necklaces which hid the slight scrawniness of her neck. The maids of honour, scurrying breathlessly to and fro, found the painted ivory fan from Italy that the Queen wanted, the leaf-green prayer book which showed off her Grace's long white fingers, loaded with rings, and the jewelled pomander stuck with sweet cloves.

They watched their handiwork greet the dazzled Ambassador with pride.

'She looks a dream – and what an actress she is!' exclaimed Bess to Frances. 'See how all the impatient lines are smoothed from her face, and her voice is full of feminine allure. Once she is in front of an audience – any audience – she ceases to be an old woman dressed like a young one, and becomes twenty-five again!'

'Well may she do so,' muttered Meg bitterly. 'For I'm sure she's stolen ten years off my life. When I brought her the wrong fan and she rapped my knuckles with it I got so flustered I almost burst into tears.'

'You need a calm disposition to deal equably with her Grace,' laughed Bess. 'Look at me – searching through that mound of jewels for one particular headdress. But did I panic?'

'Yes!' accused Meg. 'You just didn't show it in your face. You were lucky, too. Just as she was beginning to lose patience and shouted at you to bring the circlet quickly, you found it! "Here it is, Madam," you say as if butter wouldn't melt in your mouth, and that made her Grace smile and forget to rate you for taking your time.'

When the audience was over the Ambassador passed amongst the maids of honour in the Presence Chamber and was heard to mutter in wondering tones, 'What a woman! Superb! She moves with such grace. No one would take her for a day over thirty.'

When the girls repeated to their Mistress

the Ambassador's remarks, she was suitably gratified. But the session had been a tiring one. She thought she would change into simpler, more comfortable garments.

Stifling sighs, the maids of honour at last found the dress she favoured. A green gown open-fronted with a cinnamon-coloured kirtle, a circular ruff in saffron-tinted lawn and a bolster farthingale, more comfortable than the wire frame she had worn under the full skirts of the State dress.

At last they were able to settle their Mistress in a comfortable chair in the Privy Chamber to talk affairs of State with Burghley.

Then the maids of honour went out into the gardens. All except Bess, that is. She lingered amongst the Queen's wardrobe, making sure that everything was in its place, grateful for the quiet after the hectic job of dressing and re-dressing her Grace.

The room was warm – stuffy, thought Bess. A bumble bee had strayed in through a window that was opened a crack and Bess, laughing at it, opened window after window, letting in the fresh air and trying to chase the fat brown busy-body out into its natural element.

'You mistook the colours for flowers, didn't you?' Bess asked the bee. 'It's understandable, for they are brighter than many a flowerbed, all these fine dresses. But satins, silks and taffetas don't have the sweet taste of the honey from an honest rosebud, do they?'

She guided the noisy flustered creature towards an opening, leaning on the sill to watch it fly busily down to the nearest blossoms.

Meanwhile, Sir Walter waited until his Mistress was fully involved with Lord Burghley. Then he slipped into the gardens. He could hear the clear young voices of the maids of honour and, seeking them out, walked amongst them. But all the while his eyes were searching.

Where was she, the beautiful girl with the wicked sparkling blue eyes who had taken his fancy yesterday? He was thirty-five, too old – and too experienced – to be attracted by mere beauty. He had seen something in that girl's face that made him want to know her further, yet, so far, he hadn't even succeeded in learning her name.

He wandered restlessly through the gardens, then went into the palace again. Suppose she was in the maidens' dormitory? He could not gain access there. But her last job had been in the royal wardrobe. There seemed no reason why she should linger amongst the many and elaborate toilettes owned by her Mistress, but he thought he would take a look.

He opened the door of the long room,

blinking in surprise at the colours. Dresses, petticoats, kirtles, hoops and ruffs in every shade dazzled the eye, making even the sunshine appear dull in comparison.

When his eyes were accustomed to the glare, he saw the girl, standing with her back to him, apparently trying to put a bumble bee out of the window. He could hear the murmur of her voice as she talked to the insect and watched her downward gaze as her task was successfully accomplished.

He walked softly across the floor, but the slight whisper of the rushes betrayed his presence. The girl turned swiftly, a flush warming her cheeks as she saw him.

'Sir Walter, you shouldn't be here, in the Queen's robing room,' she said reproachfully.

'Shouldn't I? Why not? I'm searching for Essex. He hasn't returned to the Queen's side. She wonders where he is. I merely try to gratify her whim and discover his whereabouts.'

His eyes laughed at her whilst his lips remained grave.

Bess giggled. 'You expected to find him here?' she said politely.

'Why not? He's always hiding behind some woman's skirts. How can I tell whether he prefers the skirts full or empty?' parried Ralegh swiftly.

Bess laughed outright.

'Oh, I'll put your mind at rest, sir. He prefers a woman in a gown – until he can persuade her out of it.'

Ralegh said curiously, 'Do you speak from experience, blue eyes?'

The blue eyes flashed. 'My name is Elizabeth Throckmorton, sir. And I speak from the experience of others. I'm no lie-beside for a popinjay like Essex.'

'I'm surrounded by Elizabeths,' complained the deep Devon voice. 'Throckmorton, you said. I've heard your friends call you Bess, so I'll do the same.'

'I'll call you mad, if you treat me with friendliness before her Grace,' interrupted Bess, speaking quickly.

Ralegh took a step forward and caught her arms. 'Is it a sin to want to know you?' he asked, grinning down at her. 'You're pretty, witty and fresh as a nosegay. You neither simper, nor are you bold. I'll do you no harm, Bess.'

Bess removed his hands carefully from her sleeves. 'Harm can be in the mind, Sir Walter. Do you think her Majesty would do me no harm if she knew I was alone in here with her "Sweet Water"? And you'd soon be out of favour if you showed too much interest in me. I'm dangerous company for a gentleman who seeks the Queen's favour, sir. I'm Sir Nicholas Throckmorton's daughter.'

The black brows rose enquiringly. 'The ambassador, you mean? So I knew. And what difference does that make to how the Queen regards you?'

Bess wrinkled her white forehead, trying to think how best to put her feelings and thoughts into words.

'Whilst she has no cause to remember the past, the Queen treats me as she treats my friends. But when she remembers the time of Amy Robsart's death – the letters my father wrote to Lord Burghley were shown to her Grace – they gave the Queen such a distaste for our family,' she sighed. 'Time makes many forget, but not Queen Elizabeth. So he who befriends me does so at risk.'

Ralegh nodded his understanding. 'Then how will you ever marry?' he asked curiously.

'I shall have to accept a man in whom the Queen has no possible interest. She finds my friendship with Robert Cecil quite unexceptional. She makes remarks of course – she asks how I can abide the lovemaking of a cold-eyed pigmy – things like that. But at least she doesn't say anything to his face, as she did to Sir Geoffrey when he showed too obvious an interest.'

Ralegh's face hardened. 'No one, milkmaid or Queen, shall stop me learning to know you,' he said softly. 'God's blood, that hair! I'd like to see it loose round your shoulders instead of done up in that damned prim style. And what does that gown hide? Skin like milk, I'll warrant. Rosy breasts flattened into that stiff bodice. A slim waist hidden by a great farthingale. It's a fashion to flatter an ageing figure, not show off a young one.'

'That remark is nearly treason,' said Bess, confused, her eyes on the ground. Then she raised her face and looked Ralegh straight in the eye.

'If you play with me, you play with fire, sir. I know not whether I speak like a wanton, but you could set me aflame, if I let you. Now go, before we are discovered here together.'

Sir Walter made her a courtly bow, which started Bess giggling, and turned to leave the room. As he reached the door he said over his shoulder, 'I'm willing to risk having my beard singed.'

'Like the King of Spain?' asked Bess mockingly. 'I'd singe more than your beard, Sir Walter.'

'A fig for that, my pretty wanton. I'll see you around the Court and learn to know you,' he answered. Then the door closed gently behind him.

FOUR

SECRET COURTSHIP

The months that followed were a pleasure and a pain to Bess. She continued to work hard at her duties. Her friendship with Robert Cecil remained as before. But only to Marjory did she admit the short, dangerous meetings with Sir Walter.

'You know, Bess, he got two maids of honour with child before ever you came to Court,' said Marjory diffidently. 'I know that you would not allow yourself to be dishonoured my love, but he is an older man; experienced, passionate. How long can this uneasy friendship continue before he presses for more than talk and secret meetings?'

Bess faced her friend frankly. 'He wants marriage, Marjory. And it would ruin him with the Queen's grace, I know it would. She can overlook seduction – look at Essex and poor little Phillipa – but marriage is different. And *I'm* different. If I marry her "Water" she'd never forgive either of us. Sir

Walter lives for adventure, excitement, and the Queen's favour. Take it from him and he wouldn't be the man I love. I've explained to him,' she went on wearily, 'until my mouth is tired of forming the same words.'

The two girls were talking in a quiet ante-room whilst they mended dresses which they would need for the Accession day and Christmas festivities.

Bess raised the gown she had just darned with her tiniest stitches and heaved a sigh.

'Unless I can think of some means of weaving cloth out of rushes, I'll be appearing at Court in my shift, and that will put an end to uncertainties,' she said with a laugh.

A knock came at the door and one of the other maids of honour stood there, a letter in her hand.

'It's for you, Bess, from your brother,' she volunteered as she handed the letter over.

Bess took the letter and read it rapidly, her face losing its colour and a little shocked gasp escaping her lips.

Marjory was at her side in an instant. 'Is it bad news, my love?' she enquired, putting her arm round Bess's shaking shoulders.

'My mother – she's dead. A year almost to the day since my stepfather died. I'm to go with Arthur down to the place where she lies, to hear the will read and attend the funeral. Marjory, would you explain to the Queen for me? I must be off at once, for I can't arrive there until I have bought mourning clothes. I expect Arthur will help me with money. You'll tell – everyone – why I'm gone?'

Marjory promised, nodding slightly to show her friend she understood. Then Bess whisked away to pack such things as she would need for a short stay in the country.

When she was ready she donned a thick cloak, for the weather was already turning cold, and joined Arthur. He held the reins of her mare and a groom helped her to mount. Then the two of them rode off, into the light November haze.

'I've arranged a mourning gown of black,' said Arthur presently. 'Anna is bringing it with her. We will meet her presently and you can go into our lodgings and change. Bess, do you realise we're orphans now?'

'I suppose so,' said Bess wearily. 'But what will I do, Arthur, without Mother to turn to? I spent my holidays with her, she came to Court to see me. She made me feel there was someone who cared. Now she's gone, there is no one.'

'Anna and I will be living at Mile End soon, then you will have us close at hand,' comforted Arthur. 'We hope you'll look on our house there as a second home, dear Bess. Anna is very fond of you and likes to hear all about the life and gaiety at Court.'

Bess laughed ruefully. 'I'm not likely to be

at Court much longer myself, unless I can find some clothes,' she confessed. 'My gowns are well kept and well looked after, but I promise you, Arthur, even the Queen sometimes notices that I'm not the best dressed of her ladies.'

When the will was read, however, Bess wished the words back with all her heart. Lady Throckmorton had realised her daughter's difficulties clearly for as a young bride she herself had been shabbily dressed at Court and knew the humiliations it could bring.

She left Bess all her clothes, all her materials, all her beautiful jewellery, girdles, shoes, silk stockings and scented gloves. In addition, Bess came into possession of the things Mr Stokes had left in trust for Bess when he had died. She had all her bedroom furniture from Beaumanor, even including the bed hangings, and the matching window curtains and cushions.

After the reading of the will, Bess walked round the garden with Nicky in a daze.

'Nicky, I feel so guilty,' she admitted. 'There was I, pining and worrying for new clothes to wear, and then my troubles were solved – but in *such* a fashion!'

Nicky grinned at her and squeezed her arm. 'Mother would be happier knowing of your true happiness in her gift than in thinking you felt guilty at receiving it,' he reminded her gently. 'Wear the clothes, Bess – you'll probably have to alter some of them – and wear the jewellery. And don't forget why mother sent you to Court – to find a husband.'

'It's not so easy for a Throckmorton without a dowry to tempt some young gallant into being rash,' interrupted Bess gloomily. 'Oh, I could have had my pick of nasty old widowers, I'm not denying that. But mother married for love and I mean to do the same.'

'Have you met anyone suitable?' asked Nicky with considerable curiosity. He had often wondered why his pretty, lively sister had remained unattached for so long.

'I've met someone,' admitted Bess cautiously. 'Not suitable, though. But rather than marry another, I'd die a spinster, if not a virgin!'

'You shock me,' said Nicholas, grinning down at her. 'But take my advice, pretty one! Marry before mother's bounty runs out and you find yourself once more patching old gowns and relying on Christmas presents from your brothers for new trinkets.'

'I truly love and wish to serve the Queen, Nicky,' confessed Bess, 'and yet even stronger is my desire to be in the arms of my man.'

Nicholas laughed. 'If I was the man, you wouldn't have much to say in the matter,' he declared. 'A pretty wench like you, with a figure like yours, might get snapped up by someone else. A wise man would take you whilst he may.'

Bess grinned up at her brother in the fading afternoon light.

'Oh well, I have to admit it's more my conscience of the harm I might do him than fear for my virtue that keeps him at bay,' she admitted. 'Anyway, Nicky, I hope you'll dance at my wedding even if I never become the bride of – of my love.'

'I'll dance at your wedding, sweeting. But make it soon, or I may be too old to caper. Now come in, the air grows chill and damp rises from the ground,' returned Nicholas. Holding each other's hands tightly, they went towards the lighted house, each full of their own thoughts.

Back once more at Court, Bess put off her mourning and went back to her duties wearing some of her newly acquired finery, though not without a pang as she thought of her mother who had worn these gowns so happily and bought the materials for fresh ones, knowing well that she herself would never wear them but that they would brighten the beauty of her beloved only daughter.

Sir Walter, not a man to notice a woman's apparel, had to have the new gowns, jewellery and head-dresses severely brought to his notice, when he said flippantly, 'Gilding the lily, Bess, gilding the lily. The gowns become you well, but I'm sure your apple-blossom skin would please me more.'

Blushing, Bess raised a peacock feather fan to her face and peeped at Sir Walter through it. He is handsome, she thought proudly. Why am I so fortunate to have won the love of such a man? He was fearless, gay, bold and witty. A man who could hold to her side with no glimpse of her body, and never let his eyes stray to the more lenient ladies of the Court, who enjoyed an *affaire*, and would have worn Sir Walter's favours proudly. They wouldn't have cared whether he loved them or not, as long as they were possessed by him and could boast of it.

The occasion was a ball held in the Presence Chamber at Hampton Court. It was 1588 and it seemed that the Queen must show everyone that she cared nothing for the mighty armada that Spain was preparing against her. To their joy, the Queen was too wrapped up in affairs concerning the planned invasion of her realm by Catholic Spain to notice that one of her maids of honour spent a lot of time with Ralegh.

But soon Ralegh himself was deep in preparations for war.

With Sir Walter away, getting the navy ready to sail, Bess and Marjory drew close once more.

They had always been the best of friends, but now Marjory was having tentative advances paid to her by a respectable if rather dull gentleman of the Court, and the two girls found their love-lives – so different – kept them apart. But at present Marjory's gentleman was with the army preparing to tackle any Spaniards that might land in the invasion force and Sir Walter was everywhere at once it seemed, except the Court. The two girls drew very close once more with peril seemingly so near at hand.

'Are you afraid?' asked Marjory one fine summer day when they were gathering meadowsweet and Queen Anne's lace to strew in the Presence Chamber.

Bess laughed. 'Who could be afraid, with the Queen in a mood of high optimism and the Pope openly praising Drake and saying the Armada, he fears, will be no match for the British fleet? Why, Sir Walter hasn't a care in the world except that the Queen may make him miss the fighting.'

'Essex will also miss the fighting,' said Marjory mischievously. 'The Queen cannot bear that her darling might risk life or limb aboard one of the ships.'

'I'll say this in his favour,' Bess admitted grudgingly, 'he's no coward. But as yet he hasn't suffered.'

Marjory laughed at her friend's vehemence.

'You've got your knife into the fair and glorious earl, just because he and Ralegh are at dagger drawing,' she teased. 'Is it true that they tried to fight a duel over the Queen, but she stopped it?'

'They tried to fight a duel – or rather Essex did, and Sir Walter agreed, but the Council put a stop to it,' said Bess scornfully. 'The Queen wasn't supposed to know anything about it, but she went about for a week looking like a cat that's got at the cream. She knew and she was flattered that two stupid hotheaded men would have fought for her sake.'

'How does she do it?' muttered Marjory, glancing behind to make sure they could not be overheard. 'They really love her in a way, don't they? All the poetry, and the pretty speeches, and love letters, the expensive gifts – they aren't just a sham. Men seem to be dazzled by her even when they are close to her, as are Essex and Ralegh.'

'She has charm, wit and elegance and she really does look young for her age, by the time we've finished dressing her and painting her,' admitted Bess thoughtfully. 'And yet it's more than that. Men love her, to be sure, in fact they worship at her shrine, they compete for a word of praise, they wilt under her frown. Ralegh says it's all part of her game of love that makes it possible for a woman to rule this kingdom. I think it's a kind of magic she's had since she was scarcely more than a child, and Tom Seymour went to the block for love of her.'

'She does have a kind of magic,' agreed Marjory. 'Even we feel it, don't we? She's not a woman for women, though,' she went on. 'She's happier amongst the men.'

'Who isn't?' said Bess, rolling her blue eyes roguishly. Laughing, the two friends went towards the palace.

In August, with the defeat of the Armada at sea, scurrying ignominiously before the English fleet, the Queen and her Council still feared a military invasion. So Elizabeth and the Court set forth for Tilbury, where the Queen spoke immortal and never-to-be-forgotten words to her army. Bess, standing with the other maids of honour and ladies in waiting, searched the crowds in vain for a sight of Sir Walter. Later, she learned that the Queen had allowed him to set sail once it was obvious that the Spanish Armada was running for its life, with even the weather against it.

'He'll suffer from outrageous seasickness,' Bess told Marjory. 'Why, when he crosses from the north to the south bank of the Thames for some purpose he always tries to go round by London Bridge, for even in a barge he feels squeamish!'

But the fact that her love would be suffering from *mal de mer* didn't make Bess feel any happier. What cheered her – if it could be termed cheer – was that she knew that despite feeling ill he would be in his element, knowing the elation that danger brought. For a moment she wondered if his liaison with herself had some of this elation of danger, then she shrugged the thought from her mind. One doesn't try to coldly analyse the heat that is true love, she told herself. And she knew without any doubt that, for whatever reason, Ralegh loved her truly.

Then, when the excitement had died down, the navy was brought home and the army dismissed, Leicester died.

For the Queen it was a great and at first devastating blow. He was her first love, perhaps her only true love. He had, to be sure, married Lettice Knollys against her wishes and in secrecy, but only after years of waiting for herself. Certainly he was her strongest link with the past. She and young Robin Dudley had played together as children, even sharing the same tutor occasionally. They had been imprisoned in the Tower at the same time, though not together. Now he had died working zealously for the Queen, and Elizabeth, for a while, wanted to die, too.

But the rejoicings had to go on, and the Queen had to pretend to share in her country's pleasure.

Bonfires were lit in the streets and the

common people danced in the gutters. Everyone wanted to entertain the Queen, and in public she was all smiles and gaiety. But in the private of her withdrawing chambers she took off her mask of rejoicing and was difficult, short-tempered and melancholy.

Then the young men of the Court, and the older ones too, came into their own. Essex, the Blount brothers Charles and Christopher, Ralegh and Hatton gathered round her so that for their sakes as much as her own the Queen threw off her deep sorrow. Ralegh explained to Bess that the Queen really needed him now, and that she must be patient.

Bess knew the truth of this and she was patient, only dancing with Ralegh when the Queen was obviously engaged with someone else, cutting their secret meetings to a minimum. Sometimes she thought wistfully how marvellous it must be to be Anna Throckmorton, her dear Arthur's wife. Anna had her home, an affectionate husband, her household cares and her friends around her.

She, Bess, lived on the snatched moments when another woman wasn't monopolising her man. But what a man!

Then, in the year 1589, Ralegh and Drake combined in a venture to take reprisals against Spain for the Armada. Bess said ruefully as she saw Ralegh taking formal leave of the Queen that so far as she could understand, Spain had suffered enough for their Armada. They had lost countless men and over half their fleet, besides losing the feeling that God was on the side of the righteous (Spain, of course, to Phillip II).

But later in the day Ralegh told her, holding her gently in his arms, that if he won a rich enough prize then the Queen would forgive him anything, even marriage.

'Is the Exchequer in such a bad state then?' asked Bess, half laughing, half tearful.

'It is indeed. The cost of the navy, the cost of the army – though it wasn't needed but no man could say that – have told on the Queen's purse more than on any other. No one knows better than I how she would welcome some Spanish treasure at this moment.'

Bess saw him go with an empty ache in her heart. Her man, yet not her man. Essex, who gave the Queen the slip and joined the fleet, was brought back, and when Ralegh arrived home in England without any great fortune he found Essex so firmly enthroned in the Queen's favour that he decided to go to see to his estates in Ireland.

'But you've barely arrived home, and now you're planning to be off again,' wailed Bess when he told her.

'To be at Court where Essex holds the key

to the Queen's favour is to waste time, and time is valuable,' Ralegh told her firmly. 'My estates in Ireland need me. The Irish need me, though they don't think so. If you would only marry me, you could come as well.'

But here, at least, Bess was firm. She was not going to drag him down at the height of his career, not she.

The time seemed to Bess to drag by on leaden feet. She wrote long, amusing, misspelt letters to Ireland and Ralegh replied, telling her of his life and his estates, most of which seemed to be thriving.

Then, at long last, Bess really did have something to write to Sir Walter about. For some time Essex had been dallying with one of the maids of honour, Frances Walsingham. She was the young widow of Sir Philip Sydney and she and Bess were good friends, though Frances did not confide in her when she became pregnant by Essex.

Essex had got two of the maids of honour with child and been pardoned by the Queen. Now he married Frances Walsingham secretly, but her condition soon led to enquiries and the inevitable truth came to the Queen's ears.

Furious, she banished them both from Court, and Bess wrote immediately to Ralegh adding at the bottom in her own inimitable spelling, 'Cum whome.'

Ralegh did.

FIVE

'I CHOSE YOU IN MY HAPPIEST TIMES'

'So Robert Cecil is to marry Mistress Elizabeth Brooke,' commented Marjory to Bess as they played checkers and waited for the Queen to call them to help her disrobe. 'We always thought he was plucking up his courage to ask you to be his wife.'

Bess laughed easily. 'He was practising on me,' she said teasingly.

'Do you regret losing his regard?' asked Marjory curiously.

Bess eyed her with open surprise. 'Marjory, what an odd thing to say. I shan't lose his regard, I hope he will always feel friendship for me and I certainly couldn't fail to love his Elizabeth. She's a sweet, gentle girl who will do much for his happiness.'

'I wonder how Essex goes on?' said Meg, with idle curiosity. 'Fancy the glorious Robert banished from Court! I wonder if the gall is more bitter because of all the honey that went before?'

'At least he has Frances,' said Bess. 'If he's sulking – as is only too likely – it's Frances we should feel pity for.'

'Sir Walter Ralegh should be back from Ireland any time,' whispered Marjory to her friend. 'You wrote him, didn't you, as soon as the news of the marriage leaked out? And they say the Queen has told him he must return to Court, for she pines for the sight of her "Sweet Water".'

The door of the Privy Chamber opened softly and Lady Norris beckoned the girls inside. They went quietly through the door just as a gust of wind announced the arrival of another person in the Presence Chamber. The Queen, turning wearily to greet her maids of honour, suddenly held out her arms like a girl in love.

'Oh, Water, you've lost no time,' she said affectionately. 'I was about to disrobe, for melancholy fell thick about me. But now you're here I feel better. Will you talk with me for a while before I go to my bed-chamber?'

Bess swung round, trying to stifle her gasp, but she could not stop the warm colour stealing into her cheeks.

Ralegh spoke to the Queen but his eyes rested for a pregnant moment upon Bess.

'I hurried to obey you Grace's command,' he said, moving between the maids of honour and kneeling before the Queen.

Elizabeth waved away the maids of honour. 'Go to your beds, maidens. Sir Walter and I have much to speak of,' she said, and before they knew what had happened the door was shut. For Bess, as the door closed a decision sprang fully fledged into her mind. She might have to share this man's company with her Sovereign but she didn't have to share his body. They could belong to each other in a way which no one could alter, once he had possessed her.

I'm a wanton, thought Bess, undressing for bed, but I don't care. Waiting for the royal approval of our marriage would mean waiting for ever. Marrying in secret would mean disgrace and banishment. I'll lie with Ralegh if *I* have to be the seducer, she thought with a secret smile. She would see him the following day and tell him of her decision.

But when she and Ralegh met, strolling in one of the secluded walks of the palace gardens, it proved more difficult a suggestion to make than Bess had imagined. She had practised industriously the best way of proposing to become a man's mistress. I mustn't cheapen myself by blurting it out, she told herself severely, but when Sir Walter was beside her once more it seemed that straight honesty came easiest.

'Walter, I want you for my lover, and I

want you now. I can't bear to wait until I can legally wed you. When you are at Court you live at Durham House, not far from here. Surely I could come to you there?'

Ralegh gazed with amusement and tenderness at the embarrassed face of his young love.

'Sweetheart, you know how I've wanted you. You know how happy the Queen is with me at Court, but to have you lie with me is ever my greatest desire. Should anything happen – a child be conceived – I'll marry you at once, even if it means ruin for me with the Queen. I wouldn't have your name smeared.'

Bess was silent, leaning against his arm.

'Are you sure it's what you want?' Ralegh asked gently, seeing her face for once without its sparkling humour.

Bess nodded. 'When shall I come to you?' she whispered.

She went to Durham House for the first time the following night. Sir Walter let her in himself, by the river door where she was less likely to be noticed. Even muffled in a great cloak, Bess was shivering. Tenderly he led her to his bedchamber, trying to make her feel more at ease with teasing, casual talk of the Court.

Bess let the concealing cloak slide from her shoulders and stood before him in the plain blue gown she wore for work. Her face was pale but determined, and her hair hung loose like a curtain of heavy gold silk. Ralegh forgot his resolve to be gentle, to talk and let her choose the moment. He kissed her slender white neck whilst he pulled the gown from her.

Bess loosened her shift and let it drop round her feet. She stood before him for a moment, proudly naked, before he doused the candle and they fell together on the bed in an ecstasy of long-delayed passion.

So now Ralegh was playing a double game of love, caught between two Elizabeths – his Queen and his Bess.

Now Bess no longer felt any envy for the time the Queen kept her love from her, for didn't she have him in a way no other woman possibly could? As their love grew easier it seemed to deepen and strengthen. Bess knew too that in some way it changed Ralegh's attitude towards the Queen, making him gentler and more compassionate.

Marjory, of course, had to know. She and Bess shared a curtained-off part of the long dormitory and it was only with Marjory's help that Bess was able to escape for her meetings with her lover. Even then, she had to be back in plenty of time before the other maids of honour woke.

She couldn't go frequently to Durham House. Quite often the Queen kept Ralegh at Court too late for the excursion. Bess had to go by boat, it would have been too dangerous for a maid to roam the streets alone and she and Ralegh knew they must not be seen together. Sometimes the morning after meeting her love she was tired, her face pale, her eyes encircled with shadows. Yet this secret, dangerous love added to her beauty, giving it depth and maturity.

She had always been admired, but now more and more men eyed her with desire. Knowing this, Ralegh teased her as a temptress, wrote her poetry in which he addressed her as 'Serena', a name which suited well her broad calm brow and untroubled eyes.

> 'Now Serena, be not coy,
> Since we freely may enjoy
> Sweet embraces, such delights
> As will shorten tedious nights...'

He wrote of her 'sweet wantonness and wit', her 'eyes of light, and violet breath'. Surely, thought Bess, scanning the verses in the secrecy of her bed, no woman had ever been so serenaded by a lover!

So life went on. The placid everyday tasks around the Court, made sweeter by the breathless thrills of Ralegh's embraces.

Then the inevitable happened. Bess realised she was pregnant. She was at a loss what to do. Marjory advised her strongly against such remedies as were sold by wisewomen, but Bess would have done anything to save Ralegh from the royal fury his marriage to her would bring.

So she swallowed strange potions, which gave her stomach ache and made her vomit. She jumped off chairs and whirled round until she was giddy. But nothing availed.

Never had a woman blessed so heartily the prevailing fashion for huge farthingales as did Bess, nor had she ever so appreciated her slender figure. She remained at Court and friends said she was more graceful than ever as she paced with dignity around the corridors. Bess smiled secretly, and equally secretly found fear giving way to the satisfaction of one who carries life within her.

She didn't have to tell Ralegh, he was a man who had known other women. He noticed the slight thickening of her waistline, and though she denied strenuously that she was with child, after the fourth month denial was a mockery to one who knew her body intimately.

Sometimes they lay in bed together, Walter with his hand resting lightly on her stomach, feeling the slight flutter of the child within. Talking softly, as though the very bedcurtains had ears, they discussed this new problem. Bess felt that at twenty-six she could very well go away somewhere and give birth to the baby alone. She would bring the child up, marrying Ralegh when the right moment arose. But Ralegh was firm. She should be married to him now, in secret if she thought it politic, but marry they would.

Already the dream and glory of a pregnant woman was settling on Bess. She agreed to a secret marriage at the beginning of November and after the ceremony she rode to Mile End to her brother Arthur, whilst Sir Walter made his way down to Chatham – he was toiling hard to prepare his fleet for the voyage for which he had been begging permission for months. At last the Queen had granted that permission, and Ralegh had no intention of losing his chance to sail at last. After a few days Bess returned to Court, to find everyone buzzing with talk of the venture to seize the Spanish silver fleet and attack Panama. The Queen herself and Robert Cecil had joined Ralegh as co-sharers in the financial side of the voyage, so many people other than the sailors would benefit if the plan was successful.

Bess listened to the talk and conjecture with a smile in her heart. A smile of pride that she was married to the man who was to lead this great venture, and that inside her she carried his child.

At Christmas, Bess went to stay with Arthur and Anna, and it was agreed that she should go back to Court with various presents for the Queen and then return in

February.

During his brief visits to Court, Ralegh was so gentle and attentive that Bess told him laughingly that her secret would be out if he took such care of her.

Perhaps fortunately for them both, Ralegh was not often at Court. The work of persuading men to join the fleet, fitting out and provisioning the ship, kept him busy at Chatham.

Arthur and Anna bought expensive Christmas gifts for the Queen, hoping to soften her eventual wrath when she heard that Bess was married – and with their knowledge and approval.

Back at the palace after Christmas, Bess became aware that she was watched closely and curiously by friends and acquaintances alike. Rumours were circulating that she was no longer a maid, and it was noted – in whispers in quiet corners – that she had always shown Sir Walter Ralegh favour.

Marjory urged her to leave the Court.

'If your condition becomes public knowledge, there will be real trouble,' she warned. 'I'm told Sir Walter has had to deny to a group of friends that he has married. He won't dare tell the truth now and if your names become linked and people continue to put two and two together, I wouldn't give a groat for your chances of escaping severe punishment.'

Bess nodded. 'The atmosphere is charged with suspicion,' she agreed. 'As yet, the Queen doesn't connect the Ralegh rumours with my taste for large farthingales.' She giggled, the laughter sounding to her friend to be verging on hysteria. 'Marjory, you've been a good friend, try to stand by me when scandal attacks my name. I'll write to Arthur tonight. Would you go to the Queen and beg her to allow me to attend on my sister-in-law, who is in poor health?'

'Is Anna not well, then?' enquired Marjory.

Another nervous giggle came from Bess as she stroked her stomach significantly. 'Anna, God bless her, is well. But the tale sounds better than an admission of my sort of ill health. Oh, Marjory, I'll miss you!'

'I'll miss you as well,' agreed Marjory, tears filling her soft brown eyes. 'But perhaps you'll return to Court if Sir Walter brings untold riches to the Queen. Surely then he'll be entitled to choose him a wife.'

'Oh, I expect I'll want to be with my baby for quite a long while,' Bess said thoughtfully. 'Do you know, Marjory, I'm so looking forward to having a baby of my very own that I almost forget to be afraid.'

'Don't be afraid, Bess. You'll be in good hands, and Sir Walter will see that you have everything of the best.'

In the minds of both girls dwelt the

thought of the many young wives who died in childbed. They knew this might be their last meeting, but they didn't voice their inmost thoughts aloud. Understanding flowed between them.

'When you are acknowledged Lady Ralegh, will you live at Durham House?' enquired Marjory at last, more to give her friend's thoughts a more cheerful direction than from real interest, for she guessed the answer.

'I expect we'll live at Sherborne. It sounds a wonderful place and I love the country. As for Sir Walter, he positively dotes on Sherborne. I'm not sure he doesn't prefer it to me! He's always talking about it. He wanted to buy back his old home at Hayes Barton you know, but the owner, a Mr Duke, wouldn't sell. So he has thrown his heart and soul into Sherborne. He has already started building there, and even planting potatoes and tobacco, though the gardens are scarce set out,' she added with a rather watery laugh.

Marjory leaned forward and kissed her friend lightly on the cheek.

'Go you and get ready for your journey to Mile End. You'll ride the mare your father gave you?'

Bess nodded, her eyes roaming wistfully around the maidens' dormitory that she would know no more.

'I'll go now and speak to the Queen. When I have time I'll arrange for the bulk of your property here to be sent after you. Go now, and Godspeed.' Marjory lifted her hand in a half wave, and disappeared in the direction of the Privy Chamber.

It wasn't far from Court to Mile End. During her time in London, Bess had come to know Anna well and liked her. Perhaps fortunately for Bess, Anna didn't have a jealous bone in her body. She stayed placidly at home while Arthur visited his sister at Court, or took her to the play, or for long rides out into the country.

But now, when her opportunity of theatre-going should have been greatest, all the theatres were closed. An epidemic of the plague had swept through London and it was deemed wiser, all through 1592, to keep public places, and particularly theatres, shut.

In common with the theatres, other places of entertainment – bear gardens, cockpits and the like – were closed also.

So rather than dwell too much on the coming event, Bess began, tentatively, to learn about housekeeping from Anna. She followed her sister-in-law about the house, helping where she could and hindering only by her efforts to please. She watched little Mary toddling round the room playing with her dolls and her spinning top and tried not to remember that Mary was Anna's fourth daughter – the first three had died at birth or shortly afterwards.

Friends came to visit the house of course, but Bess kept out of the way unless they were specially close friends of her own or Sir Walter. One frequent visitor was Lady Essex, formerly Frances Walsingham. The Throckmorton and Walsingham families had always been friends and Bess and Frances had kept up a lively correspondence after Frances had been banished from Court. Although Frances was still not allowed to visit the Court, she knew all the gossip and related it to Bess with great gusto, aware that her visits brought comfort to her friend now living in such seclusion after the gaieties of Elizabeth's court.

'I may have had to promise that man-eating tigress I wouldn't go to Court,' she said gaily to Bess, 'but I refuse to stop visiting all my friends just to make her Majesty feel I am being well and truly punished for gaining Essex's affection.'

'Don't call her a man-eating tigress,' protested Bess, half laughing. 'She can't help liking our husbands – we like them ourselves. And, after all, she has only the thoughts of them to keep her warm in bed, we have something much more substantial.'

'Aye, that's true,' agreed Frances, eyes twinkling. 'Anyway, I'd rather live in seclusion like a nun than spend more time than I have to with my mother-in-law.'

'Isn't Wanstead big enough to house you both?' laughed Bess. She had heard from Arthur, who was friendly with Robert Devereux, about the Earl's palatial home.

Frances smiled ruefully. 'That *woman*, Bess. The only thing we have in common is that the Queen hates the pair of us. But as for husbands, my mother-in-law is truly the Queen of Hearts in *that* field, for what must she do but wed with young Sir Christopher Blount, who's the same age as Robert – and a good friend of his, too. It's quite ridiculous!'

The two girls crowed with mirth. 'The much-married Lettice Knollys,' gasped Bess at last. 'She's a niece of Anne Boleyn, isn't she? Gracious, what a family they are for men, for Elizabeth, virgin though she may be, still likes a man about her, and how many were beheaded for Anne Boleyn? Five?'

'It's all very well for you,' grumbled Frances. 'You look like pulling the wool over the Queen's eyes. It's too late for me, I'm out of favour for ever. Just keep cheerful, and as soon as you're delivered put the child out to nurse and go back to Court. Then, when the moment is ripe, Walter should ask for your hand in marriage. It matters little that the Queen will rage. If she consents she need know nothing of the previous affair. If she refuses...' she shrugged. 'You'll have to go through a ceremony of marriage anyway and risk her displeasure. But, believe me, nothing infuriates her more than to know she has been deceived. That was our great fault – Robert's and mine. I truly believe that if he had asked permission to marry there might have been a great fuss – well, there would have been a fuss, knowing the Queen – but nothing like the disgrace and screechings her Grace pounded our ears with when the truth came out.'

'I thought the tale was that it was our honour the Queen was so eager to protect, not our entry into the married state,' laughed Bess.

'God's blood!' gasped Frances when they had finished laughing. 'Maids of dishonour would suit the Queen's Grace better if she could only be sure they wouldn't marry her favourites but merely bear them bastard children.'

Ralegh, meanwhile, slaved over his ships and paid flying visits to his wife. Once more the couple exchanged loving letters, but could see very little of each other except for their brief clandestine meetings when Ralegh came to Court to report to the Queen and managed to steal a brief hour at Mile End with Bess.

Then, towards the end of March, Bess and

Anna were sitting together, making small garments. Bess was just saying bitterly 'I don't believe I'm going to have a baby after all. It's just a monstrous attack of wind or one of the swelling sicknesses' when she felt the first stirrings of discomfort low in her back.

She didn't say anything to Anna. This was her first child, and she wanted to make quite sure that she was in labour before she told Anna her suspicions. However, after about an hour there could be no doubt about it. The savage clawings at her back were the beginnings of childbirth.

She told Anna quietly, but Anna had lost her first three babies and was in great fear that, left alone, she might panic. She sent a servant for the midwife and hustled Bess to her bedchamber. There, she knotted a sheet to the bedpost and soon had maidservants scurrying for hot water, cloths and a cup of hot wine to keep Bess's spirits up.

Bess lay on the bed and watched the preparations with round, frightened eyes. The midwife arrived and told Bess that a first baby was often some time a-coming. Bess scowled and allowed the sweat to be wiped from her face and neck by her anxious sister-in-law.

Arthur was from home, attending to some business concerning the lease of one of his estates. When he returned home late that night it was to find his sister still struggling to give birth to the child.

For two long days and nights, Bess fought for her baby's life and her own, her lips set, every thought concentrated on the task in hand. The women were in and out of her chamber, Anna very pale. Arthur waited outside, a prey to miserable uncertainty. Little Bess, the only girl-child his mother had born, was giving birth herself, and he couldn't help her. He could only wait.

On the second day he dined miserably alone and went and stood outside the chamber where his sister lay. He heard a sharp cry, then a chuckle from the midwife accompanied by a thin wail.

Anna came out into the corridor and beckoned him into the room. Bess lay on the bed, deathly white and exhausted. For a moment she did not notice him entering the room, then her lashes stirred and she said faintly, 'It's a boy, Arthur. A son for Walter.' Her head moved wearily on the pillow to catch another glimpse of the firm wriggling body of her firstborn, then she slept.

Arthur tiptoed from the room and made an entry in his diary, so faithfully kept.

'29th March. My sister was delivered of a boy between two and three this afternoon. I wrote to Sir Walter Ralegh and sent Dick the footman, to whom I gave 10s.'

The warmly wrapped child slept in its

wooden cradle. On the fourposter, Bess lay drowned in slumber.

But Dick was already on his way to Chatham, bearing the glad tidings to Sir Walter that his wife and son were alive and well.

SIX

DECEPTION

Bess was sitting up in the fourposter, giving suck to her son. The sunlight fell brightly on the richly coloured bedcurtains and her rounded breasts, and on the face of the baby, but he was concentrating on the task in hand. He kneaded and pressed his mother's breast rhythmically, as a puppy would, encouraging the flow of milk whilst Bess softly stroked his dark mossy head with her free hand.

Anna, entering the chamber, smiled at the pleasant picture made by mother and son. Now that she had recovered from the long, exhausting labour, Bess had regained her serene beauty, her hair once more shone with health and her skin had the added flush of fulfilment.

'Bess, the christening has been arranged,' said Anna quietly, not wanting to break into Bess's happy moment with her child.

'Arthur and I will stand godparents, and the Earl of Essex also, to give the child a noble start in life.'

Bess smiled gently, still caressing the silky head within the circle of her arm. 'That is good of you, considering the feelings the Queen will bear towards my little one,' she said gratefully. 'And after the christening?'

'My love, you'll have to send him out to nurse. You haven't enough milk for him. See, already he's bruising your breast in his hunger.'

'But – but Walter hasn't seen him yet,' protested Bess.

'No, it would be too dangerous at the moment. Arthur suggests you send the child to Enfield, to our cousins the Middlemores. They will see that he is safe, never fear. What are you going to call him?'

'Damerei Ralegh,' replied Bess proudly. 'He's no ordinary child, so he'll have no ordinary name. But oh, Anna, what shall I do when they take him from me?'

'Take the advice of your friend Frances, the Countess of Essex,' pleaded Anna urgently. 'Return to Court as though you had indeed been taking care of me during the course of an illness. It's your only hope of keeping the whole affair quiet.'

So, sick at heart, Bess parted from her child on 27th April, barely a month after his birth, and went back to Greenwich. Only

Marjory knew her secret, though Bess sometimes thought the Queen looked at her coldly as she met her eyes in the mirror when she was helping to dress her mistress.

Whenever they could, Marjory and Bess talked of the small boy-child, with his dark blue eyes and milky innocence. Marjory realised that, for the first time, someone rivalled Sir Walter in Bess's affections.

It was a dangerous time for Bess at Court. She was aware that Essex, in high favour once more, could afford to keep her secret. But would he? One day, when he felt petulant or angry with Ralegh, would he forget his friendship with Arthur and his vows of secrecy, and blurt out the truth? So to protect herself a little she took a care and a pride in her dress, flirted with anyone who chose to make her the object of his gallantry, and ignored rumours for the reason for her long absence with disdain.

But somehow, Court life had lost its appeal. However hard she tried, Bess couldn't forget her baby, far away from her. She hated the feeling that she was constantly being covertly watched, even by those who professed to be her friends.

In May, Ralegh came up to London on official business but really to see his little son. Bess went down to Enfield riding pillion behind Arthur, and they brought Damerei back to Durham House to see his father. Ralegh was as enchanted by the boy as was his wife, but Bess was worried by the fact that he seemed to have grown very little since she had last seen him.

'He was such a greedy, growing child,' she said to the nurse who had accompanied them. 'What reason then for his lack of growth?'

The woman shrugged, made surly by the implied criticism.

'The plague is rife in London, though at Enfield we be luckier. Mayhap he was weakened by being born in the plague district.'

'That's nonsense,' said Bess calmly. 'If so, he wouldn't have grown and thrived whilst he was with me at Mile End. Is he well? Eating properly?'

The nurse, regretting her tone, remembered that this girl was paying her to look after the child and assured her, in what were meant to be reassuring accents, that Damerei was eating well and growing as he should.

'Babes that grow fast early on often slow in their growth as they become more active,' she said in her most authoritative manner.

When the nurse and Damerei had gone, accompanied by Arthur, Walter tried to comfort his wife. But she would only cry against his doublet that she was a bad mother to leave her babe and that without her the child would surely die.

When Ralegh had to leave her, Bess made her way back to Court, trying to comfort herself with the thought that Damerei was certainly safer out at Enfield than in the city, where the plague was a constant threat to everyone. But she couldn't forget his big eyes in his small pale face and many a night her pillow was soaked with tears.

Missing her son and her husband, she dragged through the days, telling herself that not only Damerei but Walter too would now be safe from the plague. On board the flagship sailing for the Indies surely they were safer from disease than in the growing heat of the unhealthy city? But Marjory had warned her, wide-eyed, that it was common knowledge amongst the Queen's intimates that Sir Walter Ralegh had married one of the maids of honour in secret, and rumour was once again linking their names.

'There has been no mention of a child?' asked Bess uneasily, and felt relieved when Marjory was able to assure her that none suspected anything of that nature.

Ralegh, for his part, was convinced that silence and, if needs be, denial was their best course. His ships had not yet sailed and when Robert Cecil accused him obliquely of a secret marriage, or thoughts of such a thing, he denied it vehemently.

Bess felt herself now to be in a truly uncomfortable position. To keep silence was wrong perhaps, but to deny her marriage and her child was blasphemy to her. She had wild ideas of going to the Queen and admitting she had a child, hoping that she would gain the Queen's forgiveness. She needn't say whose child – but then her courage failed her. Ralegh would hear of it, come forward and admit everything and who knew whether either he or the Queen would forgive her for the impulsive action?

Driven hither and thither like a coursed hare by her fears, Bess felt scarcely surprised when she received an urgent letter from Enfield. It was the beginning of August and the Queen was arranging a Progress, so the maidens' dormitory was littered with packing. She opened the missive with trembling hands, then sank down on her bed, her face ashen.

Bess's little son was dead. He had died a week before of the sweating sickness.

Within a week a dazed and broken Bess was imprisoned in the Tower. In another part of that mighty prison languished her husband. She managed to get a message to him telling him of their son's death. Thus there was no evidence that he had done more than marry her secretly, and even that could not be proved.

In prison, Bess was not miserable. She felt as if the worries had been taken from her shoulders. In a strange way she seemed to be paying for the sin of wantonness. She no longer accused herself of being the cause of Damerei's death. That was something that happened all too often to young babies. Her sin was that she had lain with Sir Walter before marriage and that then they had kept the marriage a secret from the Queen.

She could not help feeling a little thrill of pride, too, that she was now acknowledged, however unwillingly, by the title of 'Lady Ralegh'. But she was allowed no visitors, though she could write and receive letters, and the Queen ignored her as though she had never existed.

The Queen must indeed have been fond of Sir Walter, Bess thought, with a pang of pity for the older woman who could never know true love. So she didn't pine in prison but thought and planned for Walter, writing to Robert Cecil to do what he could in remembrance of their old friendship.

Robert Cecil was in a dilemma. Here was Essex back in favour (and Essex had never found much to please him in the unprepossessing 'cub of the old leviathan'). On the other hand he couldn't help envying Ralegh and feeling that the Tower was the right place for him – for a time at any rate.

Ralegh had everything. Health, strength, striking good looks and now Bess, the first girl young Cecil had ever loved. Cecil promised to do his best for Sir Walter with his tongue in his cheek, though he hated to think how Bess must be suffering. He did not know that her anguish was not only for Sir Walter but for the little dead son whose name must never now be spoken.

But as the days lengthened into weeks, Bess found herself sunk into occasional fits of melancholy. If only there was someone she could confide in, tell about her baby who had been so fine and strong. Then when the full sense of her loss burst upon her she would sit and weep bitterly, pressing her hands to her waist that was now so small and barren.

Then, on the 7th September, the voyage over which Ralegh had 'toiled so terribly' and then been unable to lead, came home to roost. They had captured a big East Indian carrack, the *Madre de Dios*, with an immense cargo of spices, drugs, silks, calicoes and damasks. There were rich gems on board, fine porcelain, musk and amber. The sailors got out of hand and so, alas, did many of the good people of Dartmouth. Cecil, urged on by the Queen's fury when she heard of the looting, went down to the West Country along roads smelling of musk and spices, to try to reason with the men who were despoiling the prize.

But the wily Cecil was no leader of men. He could not persuade the looters to give up one particle of their booty. In despair, he begged the Queen to release Ralegh from the Tower so that he might try his hand at getting back the treasure from the people. 'He's a remarkable man,' Cecil said to George Carew. 'He's the only one, too, who knows the proper claims of everyone concerned, including her Grace. Surely she will realise it is in her own best interests to release him, even if only temporarily.'

So the Queen was petitioned and rather than see her share of the treasure fall into other hands released Ralegh from the Tower in the charge of Sir George Carew.

Ralegh rode through the countryside, excited to be free and smell the crisp autumn air. He was greeted cheerfully by people along the way, but the sailors went mad to see him and willingly gave up their booty – which was being cheated out of them by cleverer men than they – for their rightful share.

Ralegh gazed with awe at diamonds the size of walnuts, crosses encrusted with gemstones, fifteen tons of ebony, and all the lesser treasures, including an immensely valuable cargo of pepper.

But what thrilled Ralegh most of all was the welcome he received from the common sailors and the indignation he heard whispered on every side that a man like him should be sent to the Tower for 'loving a wench too well'. It gave him hope that both himself and his Bess might come off more lightly from their troubles than he had at first supposed, for he knew how jealously the Queen regarded the love of the people.

Robert Cecil wrote to Lord Burghley telling him of the tumultuous welcome Ralegh had received and of the work he was putting in, dividing up the vast store of valuables and seeing that each got his share.

'I suppose I shall have to sacrifice my own part of the prize,' Ralegh sighed to Cecil, 'in order to buy my freedom from the Tower – and thus eventually the freedom of my Bess.'

Cecil was forced to agree. 'Don't be bitter that you have put all your money out and got practically nothing in return,' he urged Sir Walter. 'You might easily have languished in the Tower whilst your estates returned to nature and Bess grew old. As it is, this treasure will win your freedom and soon you and – er, Lady Ralegh will be able to go together to Sherborne.'

'Ah, Sherborne,' sighed Ralegh. 'I long for Bess to see it. I know she'll love it as I do, Cecil. And we'll have children,' he went on. 'I've always loved children. I'm nearly forty, it's high time I settled down with my wife at my side and our children at our knees.'

'Aye indeed, married life is good,' agreed Cecil. 'But you'll no doubt want to go back to Court once her Majesty has had time to forgive? Perhaps the Queen will have Bess back as a lady in waiting.'

But Bess, still cut off from friends and relations in the Tower, could have told Cecil how wrong he was. For her now, she knew, she would get from the Queen at best no acknowledgement of her existence. At worst, implacable hatred.

In the Tower the days passed slowly. True, she knew Sir Walter was out and doing. The ban on her seeing anyone had been lifted and she saw Arthur and her friend Marjory occasionally. From them she learned that even if he was not in the Queen's favour, at least he was her indispensable tool. But to Bess herself there seemed no end to imprisonment. She improved her needlework, she wrote lively letters to 'Sur Wattar' as she always spelt his name, and she dreamed of freedom.

One day Marjory came to visit her and told her she would soon be free to join her husband.

'Sir Walter has begged that you may leave the Tower in order to go through a ceremony of marriage with him,' she told her friend with twinkling eyes.

Bess hugged herself with excitement at the thought of seeing her husband again, and the thought of freedom, too, from those damp, confining walls.

'Will you go to Durham House, Bess, and

meet Sir Walter there?' asked Marjory.

Bess felt unaccountable fear rise in her throat. Unconsciously one hand strayed to her waist. She shook her head.

'No, I feel sure the Queen would rather I was well out of sight of the Court. I'll go to Sherborne. I expect Walter will go there as soon as he is able as he is still out of favour with her Grace. It's not fair, really, Marjory. He made sure the Queen got great riches from the *Madre de Dios*, and he had nothing but the work, yet she still does not wish to see him. So he is building within the old castle walls at Sherborne. Oh, Marjory, it's so exciting to think that at last I shall see not only my beloved Walter but his home that he is so proud of.'

The day of her release came at last. On Friday, 22nd December, just in time to celebrate Christmas, Arthur met Bess as she was brought from the Tower. He kissed her fondly, loaded her with presents for her new home which he put in a hired coach, then Bess and a trusted footman rode out of London to be met on the outskirts by Sir Walter, who held her tight and kissed her, pouring out all his relief at her release and his love for her.

Together they rode to Sherborne, which was to be the only real home Bess was to know for a long time to come.

'Our first Christmas together, dear heart,'

Ralegh said as they piled logs on the fire blazing on the hearth and sat down, hand in hand, to gaze into the dancing flames.

'Oh, Walter, there's such a lot to do here,' Bess enthused, leaning her shining head against his broad shoulder. 'I've to learn to be a good housewife for you, I shall make pots of shining jelly from the fruits growing in the garden and I'll collect honey from the hives, and make the floors shine with beeswax, cut all the sweetest herbs for our bedchamber, and...'

'I thought you had no desire for a settled life, that you wanted the Court, and London,' teased Ralegh, but he looked a little disturbed. He was happy enough at the moment, but he also knew his own nature well enough to realise that happiness with him could only last where there was action, and that one day he would long once more for the heady excitements of the Court, where he was both loved and hated.

Bess smiled up at him.

'I suppose it was the baby,' she said thoughtfully. 'Giving birth changed me in some way, just as being a mother changed me. Then, when Damerei died with me so far away, I changed again. I want your love as long as my life may last, but I want to be a mother again – the mother of your child, legally acknowledged. Somehow, London and the Court seem like a dream – nice enough whilst it lasted, but not to compare with real life. Now I want to try my hand at gardening, housewifery – and loving!'

'You'll soon have another child, my bird,' comforted Ralegh, fondling the silky skin of her bare shoulders. 'Until then we'll work together to make Sherborne a proper home for ourselves, our children and their children. And we'll speak no more of Damerei if you please, love. It's too dangerous.'

Bess sighed and leaned once more against Ralegh's shoulder. 'Will *you* go back to Court?' she enquired presently.

Ralegh laughed harshly. 'No chance of that. I'm banished from her Grace's presence for my "brutish offence" in marrying you without Gloriana's permission. Not even flattery has swayed her. No, I'm a stay-at-home husband, sweeting, until Elizabeth relents.'

Bess sighed with relief and reached up to fondle the crisp curly black beard.

'You've got your maps, globes, books. You can plan your next expedition when we're not building and making the garden,' she said contentedly.

Ralegh nodded and after a short pause said diffidently, 'You know my friend Hariot? I'd like to have him near me – I miss the talks and the arguments. And I'd like to have Marlowe for a stay – and Spencer—'

'Wait, wait,' interrupted Bess, laughing. 'I

know little of Hariot. He wasn't often at Court. But what I did hear wasn't greatly to his advantage. The talk went that he was an atheist. And Marlowe – he's a common spy!'

'He's a spy for money perhaps,' admitted Ralegh grudgingly. 'But he's a great poet – did you ever see "Tamburlaine"? It's a play of his. Marvellous.'

'He's a known hothead and a trouble-maker. Never opens his mouth without offending somebody. But if he's a friend of yours, my love, of course he's welcome to our home,' said Bess peaceably.

'You're not only the prettiest, wittiest wife a man ever married, you've got a tender heart,' smiled Ralegh, stroking the shoulder under his hand. 'Now let's forget about them. Take down your hair, my bird. I never tire of seeing it tumble around you.'

Bess, laughing, unpinned her hair and took out the pad over which the front hair was draped. Then she undid the chignon at the back and shook her head. Ralegh caught his breath as the heavy scented mass of gleaming hair fell across his hands. He pushed his fingers up through the thick strands and then held her face still for his kisses. Bess, responding, was swung off her feet and carried, laughing, through the door and up the stairs.

An interested maidservant, watching the scene from the shadows of the big hall, reported to her fellow servants that, 'The master can't keep his hands off her. And lovely she is, too. He carried her up the stairs in his arms like a baby, with all that long gold hair hanging over his arm like a cloak.'

Bess privately thought her Walter was like a magnificent god. Ralegh, caressing her warm satiny skin, knew she was the most beautiful woman he had ever possessed. But with Bess in his bed he forgot there had ever been any women before her. He forgot every woman but her. Even the remote, unattainable goddess, Gloriana, Diana, Cynthia. The woman known by so many names had lost for ever the tormented heart of her once fervent admirer, Sir Walter Ralegh.

In his love for Bess, Sir Walter knew perfect physical and mental happiness. For a while he was content to stroll beside her through the grounds, marking out the walks, the gardens, the orchards, even where walls should be built to support the fan-shaped delicacy of peach trees. Then, when he tired of this, he went indoors and wrote long letters of advice (probably, he told Bess ruefully, unwanted advice) to the Queen and Robert Cecil.

When a Parliament was called in February, with the aim of raising more money for the war in the Netherlands, Walter asked Bess to accompany him to Durham House whilst he was representing the borough of Mitchell in the House of Commons. Bess longed to go with him, but felt he stood a better chance of gaining the Queen's favour if he went alone.

He wrote to Bess constantly whilst he was away and she also corresponded with Elizabeth Cecil, now the proud mother of a son. It was she who told Bess that Ralegh was popular in the Commons and not slow to speak on behalf of the poor, despite the way the common people had treated him in the past.

Bess didn't find the time too lonely. Her personal maid, Myers, was a lively young woman not much older than her mistress, and together they explored the potential of their new home.

Then one day in April, when Bess was picking early primroses and violets for the great porcelain bowl in the hall, she heard Walter's familiar voice and, turning, flew down the path towards him.

'My dearest love! Oh, how I've missed you. Hold me tight,' she cried, whilst Ralegh swung her off her feet and covered her face with kisses.

'Are you sure you are with child?' he demanded presently. Bess turned her candid blue eyes to his face.

'Indeed, I am sure. I pray to God that this time...' she turned away, biting her lip.

Ralegh stood behind her, resting his chin on her head with his arms round her waist. Together they gazed out over their estate, already growing so fair and noble with the spring green blurring the outlines of the trees and bushes.

'Don't *worry*, my bird. This time all will go well. The birth will be easier, and you will keep the boy by you so that none shall be able to neglect him. I expect he'll be sadly spoiled.'

'Suppose it's a girl?' enquired Bess, turning in his arms to gaze into his face.

'Then we'll call her Elizabeth and I'll swear she's named for the Queen,' Ralegh replied promptly, a wicked smile tilting his moustache. 'That might ensure me a place at Court – or in the Tower, I'm not sure which.'

Hand in hand, they turned to walk back towards the house.

'She has shown you no favour, then?' Bess enquired without much hope. Ralegh shook his head.

'Essex is all. He rules her heart and Robert Cecil rules her head – or as much as any man can,' he added with a grin.

'The tide will turn for you, my love,' comforted Bess. 'She must realise that you have affection for her but all Essex wants is a key to her treasure chest – and I mean that literally,' she added, twinkling up at him.

100

'Oh, Bess, I've brought dear Spencer down with me for a few weeks. You'll like him, I know. Such a brilliant, gentle fellow, my bird. Be kind to him, for he's shy and ill at ease with women. He's only a lad really.'

Bess giggled. 'Oh, Walter, every time I think of Edmund Spencer I remember the Queen giving him a pension of fifty pounds a year on his return from Ireland and old Burghley, with his money and estates grubbed from heaven knows what sources, grumbling to himself "So much, for a song!" We all laughed at him when he'd gone, mean old man.'

Ralegh laughed too but said reprovingly, 'Not mean, Bess. He's very generous with his own money. He's just careful with the Queen's purse, which has so many more demands on it than she can meet. That's his job.'

'Yet he never refuses the gifts she bestows on him,' reminded Bess slyly, and they were both still laughing when they entered the room where Spencer awaited them, standing self-consciously studying a picture on the wall.

As Ralegh explained the joke, Bess studied Spencer and liked what she saw. This slim, light-haired youth with the dreamy eyes and sensitive mouth would never take her Walter from her. He was a follower of men, not a leader. And he looked as if country air and country food would not come amiss either, she decided, feeling quite motherly towards him.

Bess excused herself to the men and went to explain to Smith, the cook, that she wanted good, nourishing food put before them whilst Mr Spencer was staying. Then she lingered in the stillroom, covertly admiring the neat rows of preserves and pickles the housekeeper had made last summer. Lady Throckmorton would have been so proud, thought Bess wistfully. But she had not lived to see the transformation of her tomboy daughter into the careful housewife she had become.

For by the time Bess and Walter had married, Lady Throckmorton had been in her grave a year. Sir Walter Ralegh, that proud, eager, self-willed man, had married a penniless orphan. It didn't seem to matter. It was Bess herself, her laughter, her slender limbs and lovely graceful movements and the elfin charm of her face that bound Sir Walter to her as surely now as they would do throughout their life together.

As the months passed and Bess grew more ungainly, she found she was studying her husband as one might try to discover the inner meaning in a complicated book. He was, she admitted to herself, difficult to pin down in any way. There seemed no nice tidy niche into which his personality could be put, labelled 'generous', or 'adventurous', or 'avaricious'.

She, who had only known him at Court and during their secret interludes, now discovered he had bouts of great buoyancy interspersed with deep melancholies. It seemed, thought Bess, that he must always be in the heights of delight or the depths of despair. Bess, with her more placid disposition, found this difficult to understand. Herself passionately truthful, she wished Sir Walter wouldn't tell tall stories so often that in the end he himself believed them. She knew that when it suited him he could lie better than any other man in the kingdom.

'But he never lies to me,' she murmured thankfully, going about her household tasks.

It was strange, she mused, how a man who on occasion could be such a liar could accept the word of almost every other person alive, and believe in their words implicitly. At the moment, probably the closest friends the Raleghs had were Robert Cecil and his Elizabeth. Despite their obvious unpopularity at Court the Cecils did not hesitate to pay long and happy visits to Sherborne and the Raleghs gladly accepted the Cecils' hospitality in return. Bess realised at once that these visits were made without the Queen's knowledge or consent, and that Robert Cecil, like his father before him, weighed every word, every action, in the balance before he spoke or acted.

She told Ralegh this and he laughed and teased her for getting odd ideas during her pregnancy.

Bess, responding as always to his laughter, wished nevertheless sometimes that Ralegh would follow this cautious path. Sometimes, despite his mocking laughter, she even advised him to do so. But even whilst the words were on her lips she knew that if he had been a man who thought before he spoke, and weighed his deeds by their effect on his personal fortunes, she would never have fallen in love with him.

She knew from her years at Court that Ralegh was a restless person. But now he seemed like a pent-up ball of energy, bouncing hither and thither. He would come down to Sherborne and spend happy weeks planning the garden, writing and studying in his room, supervising the building and reconstruction that seemed to be going on most of the time. He would watch over Bess, tease her about her figure, telling her that she looked like one of the ships of the Spanish Armada fleeing before the wind.

Then suddenly he would become quiet and introverted, writing dark, bitter little poems that Bess thought beautiful but which she found difficult to understand. Then one morning he would be kissing her goodbye before he chased off to visit a friend lately back from a voyage, or to speak to Cecil in person, or discover whether there was any news of his settlers in Virginia.

Bess knew, though he seldom spoke of it to her, that he was trying to get back into the Queen's favour. She thought with a little frisson of fear that perhaps one was happier away from Court and out of sight of the Queen's sharp eye.

Here, the quiet of Sherborne was disturbed only by friends. But at Court it was a constant love-battle for the Queen's favour. Now that Ralegh was married he could no longer hope for a foremost place in the lists and he had never gone out of his way to seek popularity. Those friends that he did have would be true to him to death, but the vast majority of the nobles and gentlemen who frequented Elizabeth's Court feared and despised him.

Why, why, why? she asked herself impatiently as he walked up and down, up and down, puffing smoke from his pipe, his eyes fixed on the ground but seeing – what? Why must he put himself once more within reach of the Queen's displeasure? Then she would laugh and tell herself chance would be a fine thing. Sir Walter had yet to be received at Court!

One day in late August, Bess sat in the shade of a cedar tree with her sister-in-law

Anna. Ralegh, bored by the heat and the lack of brilliant conversation, had gone hawking with Arthur, leaving the two women to the quiet garden, gentle chat, and the task of yet again sewing tiny garments.

'All these swaddling bands,' sighed Bess, finishing hemming one and laying it on the growing pile by her side. 'The lace caps, the petticoats, the crosse-clothes, bibs, mantles ... oh, Anna, the list seems never-ending!'

'They'll not be wasted,' comforted Anna with a chuckle. 'The next babe will use these little clothes when your first baby grows too big.'

Bess snorted. 'If Walter's here for long enough to give me another baby,' she said with a half sigh.

'Sir Walter is a restless man, is he not, Bess?' asked Anna presently. 'He cannot be still, no not even when he's sitting in a chair talking, for then he gestures with his pipe and keeps jumping up to illustrate his point, until I'm quite exhausted.'

'He exhausts us all,' laughed Bess, thankfully laying down the last band and fanning herself with the carved ivory fan Ralegh had given her. 'Why, at his age most men settle down happily to run their estates and manage their families. But not Walter! Oh no, he goes from pillar to post searching for – oh, excitement and adventure I suppose. But of course before he can have any of these things he must win back Elizabeth's elusive favour.'

'He seems more settled in some ways,' offered Anna. 'His dress for instance is not as fanciful as it used to be.'

'Well, Court clothes would scarcely do for Sherborne,' laughed Bess. 'What would the simple country people think if he rode amongst them in a cloak sewn with pearls which scattered as he moved? Goodness knows, the people here regard him as strange enough without adding that. They think him an atheist and say he questions the accepted ideas of the Church. Those that know him love him, but the others fear him. People are always afraid of what they don't understand, and even *I* don't really understand Walter.'

'Arthur smokes a pipe now you know,' said Anna thoughtfully, bending over her work once more. 'He admires your husband so much, Bess. But he seems to find smoking soothing to his nerves and restful. Now when Sir Walter lights up his pipe it's almost as if he sees pictures in the curling smoke, reminding him of his voyages and adventures, and making him once more restless and dissatisfied with this quiet life.'

'Yes, you've certainly found something I hadn't thought of. I suppose to Walter smoking does bring back days a-voyaging, days in foreign lands. Even the mad day he persuaded the Queen to smoke a pipe with him.' She sighed. 'With Walter everything must be questions, questions. He cannot be content to simply accept what the Church says, he must query. He's the same with everything. What makes his potatoes flourish in Ireland when they do not grow so bravely down here? Why is seawater undrinkable? Why do the waters at Bath taste strange? We're opposites, you know,' she went on seriously. 'That's why we can love and admire each other and live happily together. I'm placid, not prone to melancholy, even my worst enemy has never accused me of arrogance or vanity. But, Anna, Walter's mind is like a star beside a fire on a little hearth compared with the minds of other men. Given the opportunity he could do great things – greater by far than any he has done already.'

'In other words, a man worth losing your sleep over?' asked Anna, smiling. She had heard Bess, when Walter was from home, moving to and fro in her room, restlessly waiting for the coming of day.

'A man worth losing your life for,' said Bess promptly. 'If he wants me to risk life and limb in one of his colonies and the Queen permits, I'll go. I tell you, Anna, in this life all is chance. Our lives hang by a thread of caprice. Tomorrow the plague may take me, or I may die in childbed, so the adventuring of my body and spirit with Sir Walter in a foreign land is a small thing.'

She picked up a warm, sun-ripened peach from the bowl of fruit between them and bit into it.

'Life is sweet, but love is sweeter,' she told her sister-in-law thoughtfully.

'Yes, Sir Walter is a man to die for.'

SEVEN

MOTHERHOOD

'Is anything the matter, my bird?' asked
Ralegh.

He was sitting at the table, a great map
spread out before him, marking it here and
there, frowning awhile and scribbling notes.

His attention had been drawn from his
task by Bess, who had been sitting motion-
less for some while, gazing into the fire. It
was late October and outside the wind
brought the dead leaves whirling from the
trees and already the early mornings showed
the first crisp frosts of winter.

Bess, who was holding herself quite still,
looked at him with surprise.

'Oh, my love, I didn't want to worry you.
The pains have started. I've been timing
them by the clock on the mantel. I wasn't
going to say anything until they got closer,
they're still a good ten minutes apart.'

Ralegh leapt to his feet, scattering papers
all over the floor, and going to the door

shouted, 'Peg, you and Myers come here, and send Peter Venn to me also.'

The maidservant, closely followed by Bess's personal maid, Myers, ran into the room. Hard at their heels came the head groom, who had been warming himself by the kitchen fire.

'Lady Ralegh is in labour with the child,' Ralegh told them tersely. 'Peter, ride for the midwife. Peg, fetch Mistress Worthing from her chamber, she's writing letters there. Myers, help your mistress to bed.'

'Must we disturb Marjory?' protested Bess. 'The babe has decided to come into the world betimes, but it may be many hours before he arrives. There is no need for Marjory to be bothered yet, surely?'

'Your friend will want to be with you at such a time,' said Ralegh reproachfully. 'I, too, shall not be far away. Don't worry, my bird, soon you'll hold your child in your arms. You said yourself he's early. I expect that means he will struggle as hard as you will for release into the world.'

Peg came back into the room with Marjory at her heels. Marjory was married now, but though she had no children as yet she attended frequently on her stepmother, who had children like doorsteps, Marjory complained bitterly. As soon as one was out of swaddling bands she was beginning another pregnancy.

Now, however, she felt grateful for her experience as she hurried forward and caught Bess's arm.

'Come, my dear. Myers and I will help you out of that gown and into your bed. Then we'll be able to help the child to come forth quickly. 'After all, it's not your–' she hesitated, glancing at Myers and remembering how Bess had told her that, even between themselves, she and Walter never mentioned that first, fatal boy baby.

'It's not your job to worry now; the responsibility for your well-being is in the hands of God and the midwife,' she finished.

Bess looked at her with huge pain-filled eyes but didn't speak. Ralegh's face was inscrutable. He might have realised she had barely swallowed an indiscretion, or he might be too full of thought for Bess to remember that unhappy child in its nameless grave.

When she had settled her friend in bed, Marjory sat down beside her and talked quietly, only breaking off to wipe the sweat from the pale face on the pillow.

'It's near, Marjory, I know it's near. I wish the midwife would hurry,' muttered Bess at last.

Marjory lowered her tone to a whisper, though Myers had left the room to inform Sir Walter that the birth would seem to be imminent.

'Everyone thinks it's your first child, Bess. As you know, a first child is usually tardy. Ah, here comes your husband to cheer you.'

Ralegh tiptoed across the rushes as though silence was essential to birth, his face wearing a frightened look Marjory had never seen on it before.

'The midwife is already attending a confinement,' he whispered hoarsely to Marjory. 'But the doctor is making all speed here. Can you manage, Marjory, until the doctor arrives?'

'Certainly I can,' said Marjory, pretending to be affronted. 'Many's the child I've delivered, Sir Walter.' She turned her attention to the girl on the bed.

'There's a sheet knotted to the bedpost for you to pull on, Bess,' she said, running her eyes over the preparations she had made.

Sir Walter began to tiptoe from the room when Bess gave a hoarse, triumphant cry. 'He's coming, my love. Don't leave me.'

Her hands clung to his and she began the slow rhythmic pushing whilst her nails dug into Ralegh's hands as though holding them was to hold life itself. Marjory said quietly, 'Well done, Bess, here he comes,' and Ralegh was conscious that she was gently helping the baby as his wife pushed.

To Ralegh it seemed that the world was bound up in those two figures, bringing life into the world. To his shame his head swam for a moment, then it cleared and he saw his son born, saw Bess sink back on to the pillows with a gasp of relief.

He sat by the bedside watching the boy being washed and swaddled and put in the cradle, in a gentle daze of gratitude for Bess's safe deliverance. He thought at first she slept, then her lids slowly raised and she whispered, 'He – was – too – quick.' Marjory and Myers thrust Ralegh from the room with instructions to get the doctor to them at all costs, and then he was out in the cold with a light rain driving in his face, riding towards the doctor's house.

As he rode through the dark and rain he tried to pray. Bess was haemorrhaging, Marjory had said. His son was lying safe and warm in his cradle. He was riding alive and well through the countryside. But Bess, his life's darling, might be dying.

Ralegh never forgot that nightmare ride. When he and the doctor arrived back at Sherborne, Marjory, paler than Ralegh had ever seen her, told her they thought they had stopped the bleeding but Bess was in a faint through loss of blood.

The doctor accompanied Ralegh to the bedchamber and examined Bess as she lay apparently lifeless on the bed.

'It's alright, Sir,' he was able to tell Ralegh comfortably presently. 'Your young friend

114

has a head on her shoulders, likely she saved Lady Ralegh's life tonight. All would have been well had it not been for the size of the child and the speed of his arrival. Lady Ralegh will be weak for some months perhaps, but unless a fever should set in all will be well with her now.'

He walked over to the elaborately carved wooden cradle and eyed the occupant, smiling at the small crumpled face which still looked resentful, fringed with a lace cap and swaddled in the bands Bess had laboured over so lovingly, with lavender scented blankets covering him and warmed by the fire in the grate.

'My, he *is* a size. I don't think I've ever seen a lustier boy. Well, lad, you nearly killed your mother, who's a lady made narrow in the hips. Be sure you don't add to her troubles now by waking her with your wailing.'

As if he had heard and understood the baby began a mutter that changed to a roar when his father tried to soothe him by rocking the cradle.

'Take him into another room – one of the women of the house will look after him,' advised the doctor. 'Don't let Lady Ralegh try to feed him herself, she's too weak and he'll be a hearty one to suck. I'll send a wet-nurse up tomorrow.'

He and Ralegh picked up the cradle between them and carried it through to

Marjory's room. The firelight flickered on the carving as the two men set it down, and Peg was called to sit beside the babe whilst Marjory made Bess a posset to drink when she woke.

Ralegh thanked the doctor and saw him safely off, then hurried back to Bess. He, who had seen so many dead and dying on his campaigns in the Netherlands, who had taken part in the massacre led by Lord Grey in Ireland, now found himself so sickened by the sight of the blood which dappled Bess's smooth arms and stuck the ends of her hair into points, that he found his senses swimming.

He steeled himself and went over to the jug and ewer. When Marjory came back some ten minutes later the great Sir Walter was kneeling by the side of his adored wife, washing the bloodstains from her body, whilst tears ran unchecked and unheeded down his cheeks.

Sir Walter was never to forget his first sight of birth. When Bess was fit again and would suggest another child the memory of her sweetness clotted by blood would rush into his mind and he would make excuses. Never again, he vowed, would he deliberately get her with child. Birth control of a sort was possible and he could possess her without intentionally risking her life in that fashion again.

So little Wat, as they called young Walter Ralegh, relied for most of his youth on the companionship of his many cousins, the children of his parents' friends and the children growing up on the estate. Lack of brothers or sisters certainly didn't bother Wat. His father loved and played with him, his mother worshipped him. He was King of Sherborne. It was enough for any small boy.

In the months that followed, Bess gradually regained her former health and strength. For once, Ralegh was in no mood for 'bouncing like a ball from one place to another', as Bess had so often remarked. All he wanted was to watch over this pale girl and the child who had nearly cost him so dear.

Perhaps sacrifice deepens love, thought Marjory, as she watched them together in the early summer of 1594. For the time at any rate, Ralegh seemed content to sacrifice his hopes of the Queen's favour to watch over his sweetheart.

Wat, at seven months, could by his dress have been taken for a small girl, for he wore petticoats, a lace cap and a girdle where his handkerchief and toys were hung, just as a baby girl would. His long curls clustered like two thick bunches of black currants on each side of his face, but even at his small age few could have mistaken him for a female. He crawled everywhere with great competence, stopping occasionally to chew the coral and bells hanging at his waist, or to tear the handkerchief with his new little teeth. But if he wanted something how he yelled, marvelled Marjory. His face would screw up and turn almost purple, his mouth would open so wide one could see his tonsils and the noise was really fearsome. Marjory had noted, however, that never a tear fell from those eyes, and as soon as he was given his way the yells stopped as though an inner tap had been turned off.

Sir Walter rolled Wat's coloured woolly ball across the grass and whilst his son was in pursuit of it crept softly away towards the house, giving Marjory a fleeting wink as he did so.

Marjory walked over to her friend. She thought Bess had never looked so beautiful. She had regained her slim figure and the glow of health shone on her cheeks. She was as supple and lissom as ever; it was difficult to believe she had borne two children. The sunny days had given her pale skin the flush of a peach whilst bleaching the gold of her hair to a lighter shade.

'Bess, you look the picture of health and happiness,' Marjory told her friend as they sat together on the garden seat.

'Sir Walter took me sea-bathing at Weymouth a few weeks ago,' Bess informed her, smiling at Marjory's astonishment. 'I'm quite an accomplished swimmer, you know. Nicky taught me when I was about seven.'

'I've heard sea-bathing is healthful,' admitted Marjory. 'But I haven't tried it myself. Ugh, fancy getting all covered in salty water – cold at that! I think I'll stick to the hot waters at Bath when I feel in need of a cure.'

Bess suddenly noticed Wat's little round bottom and soft velvet shoes as he crawled rapidly across the lawn in the direction of the nearest flower border. Running after him she caught him up and tossed him, giggling wildly, into the air.

'You rascal, come back with me and play with your nice woolly ball,' she said enticingly, tickling fat baby Wat till he shook with laughter.

'He picks the heads off the flowers,' she admitted ruefully to Marjory, sitting him on her knee and letting him play with her necklace. 'It makes Walter so cross, but I keep telling him Wat's only a baby yet, he'll grow out of his destructive ways. You will, my chick, won't you?' she appealed to the baby, who waved fat fists and tugged hard at her pearl beads.

'Here comes Myers,' said Bess with relief. 'She can handle you, can't she, my poppet? Time for a nice rest with Myers, little Wat.'

Little Wat tumbled contentedly from his

mother's arms into Myers' and once again peace reigned under the shade of the cedar tree.

'Does Sir Walter have any scheme for the coming months?' enquired Marjory at length.

Bess smiled broadly.

'I've yet to know my husband when he has *no* scheme hatching. But now I'm in high health again I expect he'll be back to bothering the Cecils and the Queen about his voyage to Guiana. He's convinced himself that it's a modern El Dorado and that he'll find gold there. He's almost convinced me,' she added with a laugh.

'Do you mind him going?' Marjory asked curiously.

Bess looked at her with serene blue eyes. 'Do you mind high summer turning to autumn? Do you mind when the leaves fall and the snow comes? It's no use minding with Walter any more than it helps to worry over the seasons. I married him knowing him to be a powder keg of energy which must have freedom or explode.'

'Has he got anywhere in his hope for the Queen's return of favour?' asked Marjory.

Bess shook her head.

'No. He writes. She never even sends a line in return.'

'What else has he done?' asked Marjory, smiling at her friend's vivacious face.

'Oh, sold manors to raise money, sent to Trinidad to spy out the land. But he'll get there, Marjory, never doubt that. And whether there's gold to be found or not, he'll have the thrill of exploring new lands and I,' with a tiny sigh, 'shall wait at home and pray for his happiness and safety and speedy return.'

Bess was right. In the spring of 1595 Ralegh kissed her goodbye in the courtyard at Sherborne and rode off to Plymouth to join his small fleet of five ships. Permission had been grudgingly given at last by Elizabeth, so Bess held Wat by his leading strings whilst he waved to 'Dada', and gave herself up to waiting.

However, on this occasion she didn't wait at Sherborne for long. Sir Walter's fleet was driven back to Plymouth eight weeks later by contrary winds. He received a hasty note from Bess telling him that the plague had broken out at Sherborne and that she was taking Wat to a healthier part of the country.

'My love will be better – probably safe even – searching for his El Dorado than risking the plague at Sherborne,' Bess comforted herself as she packed two cases for herself and Wat.

Bess went to stay with Lady Essex, her dear Frances, who was also a husband lacking at the moment. The handsome, self-centred young Earl was attending on the

Queen, of course.

When she returned to Sherborne, closely followed by Wat and the faithful Myers, kind brother Arthur suggested himself as a guest for a short period, and Bess welcomed him gladly.

She was sorry to see that he had aged noticeably. Though barely forty – three years younger than Walter – he was already greying slightly at the temples and growing stout. His health had always fascinated him so that he grew rapidly boring on the state of his inside, but now it was an obsession. Bess, accustomed to living with a man who never gave a thought to his bodily functions, found something almost morbid in the way Arthur dosed himself with strange concoctions. He purged himself so regularly and with such thoroughness that she was mischievously tempted to write 'Arthur – His Seat' on the door of the privy.

'It's a good thing I've a strong stomach,' she grumbled to Myers. 'To be eating a succulent rabbit pie and suddenly to be informed that the last purging had only given Mr Throckmorton six stools is enough to put anyone off their food. I wonder Anna isn't as thin as a reed.'

Myers, chuckling grimly, said, 'He eats well enough, my lady. And his good wife would probably find Sir Walter's lack of interest in purges terrible worrying.'

'Talking of rabbit pies, Myers, do you suppose my brother would enjoy a coney shoot with one or two of the men from the estate? I feel I entertain him shabbily now that Sir Walter is from home.'

However, Arthur certainly didn't think so. He and Bess rode out together and he admired the beauty of the country round Sherborne and the way the estate was progressing. In the evenings they read plays together or Arthur showed his sister plans of the new manor he was building at Paulerspury. 'The panelling comes from Kenilworth and is very fine, very fine indeed,' he told Bess proudly.

The visit was a short one, but Bess and Wat were not left alone for long. In June, Nicholas came a-visiting, bringing Robert with him, and Bess thoroughly enjoyed entertaining her brothers, boasting about her son's prowess and watching them enjoy the excellent hunting and hawking to be had on her estate.

She saw them go with regret, tempered by the fact that Nicholas had left with her a portfolio of plays, some old, some new, for her to read during the lonely evenings until Sir Walter returned to her.

The old longing for the noise and smell of packed humanity, for the thrill of becoming caught up in the acting so that you yourself were a part of that life for a brief hour or two, tempted Bess to go back to Durham House. But she decided not to do so until Ralegh returned and then they could go to the play together.

In early September, Sir Walter returned to Sherborne, having lost three of his five ships and, despite the most arduous search, having failed to find gold or precious stones.

'It's a wonderful land – a marvellous land,' he enthused to Bess. 'But the heat is so great and the river when the rains came flooded the land so that we were in danger from every source. Fever, death by drowning, death by snakebite.'

'Will her Grace allow you to go back to Court now, dear heart?' asked Bess anxiously.

Ralegh shook his head gloomily. 'Why should she? All she cares about – *all* – is money. For her there is no excitement in strange countries and stranger customs. Colonies have no interest for her unless they show spectacular financial returns within a year or so of their beginning. She will not allow me into her presence to tell her what I found in Guiana, or how far up the mighty Orinoco I ventured with my men. The sights we saw, the fruits we discovered never known to an Englishman before, even the strangest oddity of all – little oysters growing on trees. How can she know of these things when she will neither receive me nor read my letters?'

'Why don't you write a book about it?' suggested Bess idly. 'Remember the book you wrote about the death of gallant Sir Richard Grenville aboard *The Revenge*? That was well received and eagerly read by everyone of note, I promise you.'

'I could do so, I suppose,' said Ralegh grudgingly. 'Now, when I should be gladly safe home again, all I can think of is that mysterious country, so rich in promise. To write about it might ease me a little, even if the book gave pleasure to none but myself.'

Bess gave him a wicked grin and rising from her seat kissed the tip of his nose.

'Come out of the sullens, dear heart. You have me, for what I'm worth. You have our beloved son. You have this noble Sherborne of ours, and Durham House to go to when you would be in London, near the centre of things. You'll win back to favour, never fear.'

So Ralegh began his book *The Discovery of the Large, Rich and Beautiful Empire of Guiana*, and in between revelling in writing of the beauty and strangeness of the land that was his heart's desire, he sent two further expeditions under the charge of an old friend, Laurence Keymis, a Balliol don turned adventurer and explorer. He discovered nothing, but this did not dampen Ralegh's enthusiasm.

His book was duly published and though

many people openly called it a tissue of lies and fantasy, it was widely acclaimed for the beauty and clarity of the writing.

Bess read the book with enthusiasm and sent copies to her brothers Arthur and Nicholas, whose enjoyment rivalled her own. She also sent a copy to Cecil, telling him of her pleasure in the work and of how her brothers, too, had been enthralled by such adventures.

'She's got a fine, vivid imagination,' Cecil told his wife, Elizabeth. 'It runs in the Throckmortons, you know. Her father was much taken with Mary Stuart as a young woman, and he wrote reports about her which did him no good in the eyes of Elizabeth, so my father used to say.'

'Your father showed the Queen letters meant for his eyes alone. I'd say his was the greater indiscretion,' replied Elizabeth a trifle sharply. She was uneasily aware that her husband sometimes showed letters to the Queen which had certainly never been penned for any but Cecil's gaze.

'Never mind that,' Cecil said gloomily. 'Heaven alone knows what mischief Ralegh is brewing now. You'd think he'd be content with his book and sending poor Keymis scudding off to his imaginary "El Dorado". But now he and Essex have sunk their differences and plan an attack on Cadiz. It's my belief Bess had a hand in that reconciliation. She stayed with Lady Essex when the plague was hot at Sherborne last summer.'

'I asked you if we could have her here,' reminded Elizabeth, 'but you said you were too busy for entertaining guests.'

But to Ralegh himself, Cecil took quite a different tone, encouraging and full of praise. He promised that during Ralegh's absence he would keep an eye on Bess and young Wat.

However, when Ralegh and the fleet sailed, Bess fled, too. She felt she had had enough solitude to last her for some time. She went to Mile End, where she and Anna could comfort one another for, much to Bess's secret amazement, Arthur had gone with Sir Walter on the voyage to Cadiz.

Anna found much comfort in her sister-in-law's almost childish trust in her Walter's ability to keep Arthur from any sort of harm. Anna herself was less hopeful. She knew that Arthur was powerfully attracted by the magnetic young Earl of Essex and he seemed to have a bad effect on anyone in his vicinity.

But when Anna confided her fears, Bess replied with real sincerity, 'Walter knows how Arthur and I love one another. He would scarcely dare to return to England if he had allowed Arthur to fall into unnecessary danger. We must both realise though, dear Anna, that in a land and sea battle no man can count himself safe until he is home again.'

'Oh, Bess, would that they were safe home again already,' sighed plump, comfortable Anna. 'Shall we take the children to see the lions at the Tower tomorrow? Little Wat has had so few opportunities of visiting London, I'm sure he'd love to see the beasts.'

Bess agreed, thinking with reluctant humour that had her sister-in-law a nastier nature she might well have added that the lions, also, might be glad to take a look at young Wat and perhaps a few lessons in how to *really* roar! For Anna, who loved all children, found it difficult to love such an imp of mischief as Wat. Still unbreeched, he trotted around the house holding his skirts up before him like a pretty little girl, but his temper, his actions and (occasionally) his language reminded one that he was a boy, and the son of a sailor at that!

One day, shortly after their visit to the beasts at the Tower, Bess came running to Anna, a letter in her hand.

'Robert Cecil has been appointed to the Council,' she announced gleefully. 'It had to be done with Essex absent, of course, or there would have been a great fuss, with Essex railing that the Queen doesn't trust him with State business (which, of course, is true). Oh Lord, how furious Essex will be when he returns home to find Old

Leviathan has at last got his cub on to the Council.'

'How you understand these things is beyond me, Bess,' said Anna plaintively. 'I'm too busy with my housekeeping to pay much attention to affairs of State.'

'I'm sorry, Anna,' said Bess penitently, 'but I felt I had to tell *someone*. If you were married to Walter, you would know how important these things are. Ralegh and Cecil are friends – though Cecil will only stay friends whilst it suits him, I think. On the other hand, Cecil and Essex cannot abide each other. So now we have a friend on the Council. He could, if he would, be very useful to Walter from such an exalted position.'

'Whilst it suits him to remain friends,' Anna reminded her dryly. 'Will it suit him to be friendly when (or rather if) Sir Walter returns to the Queen's favour?'

Bess sighed and gazed at the letter in her hand. 'I don't know,' she admitted ruefully. 'The only real hope of genuine friendship is that both Elizabeth and Robert Cecil are fond of *me*. It sounds conceited, I know,' she went on, 'but before he married Elizabeth, Cecil was always by my side and our friendship has continued. Elizabeth, of course, I knew as a fellow maid of honour whilst I was at Court.'

She pressed her hands to her head and

walked towards the cradle where the youngest Throckmorton daughter lay gurgling.

'It's all so difficult, so full of intrigue and subtleties and deceit,' she murmured. 'Walter is as innocent as this babe of yours over some things, Anna. If a man professes friendship, Walter believes him. He never thinks to look into the man's mind for possible treachery. But I mustn't start worrying about Court affairs. Did you know Wat has found out how to open the door of your stillroom?'

Anna, with an agitated squeak, left her seat by the cradle and rushed to the stillroom whilst Bess, giggling, followed her.

The culprit, one fat fist in a pot of strawberry preserve, waved the other cheerfully to his distracted aunt.

'Wat 'ad to stand on ve stool to weach ve plaguey 'andle,' he said thickly and a trifle reproachfully.

Anna gasped thankfully, 'Only one jar – oh, goodness, the relief! But what a state he's in. Honestly, Bess, I don't know why he doesn't drive you into the madhouse.'

'He keeps me sane,' said Bess cheerfully, picking up her sticky son and detaching the jar from his hand. 'You can imagine how much I might worry, fret with loneliness, with Sir Walter from home so much. As it is, I'm too busy following in the young master's footsteps, making sure he doesn't kill himself or someone else, to go mad with worry.'

'Well, I don't suppose Arthur will follow Sir Walter on any more of these hare-brained schemes,' said Anna as they cleaned up the small culprit. 'The country house down at Paulerspury is nearly finished. Arthur is buying furniture, a grand Turkish carpet and other fancy pieces for our very own manor house. Of course, it will be nothing like Sherborne, but Arthur said he got many of his ideas for the laying out of the grounds and gardens from Sir Walter.'

When the two brothers-in-law returned to Mile End, they got a conquering heroes' welcome from two relieved and delighted wives. The battle of Cadiz had been a great victory for the English over the Spanish, though Ralegh was annoyed with the slowness of thought that had allowed the Spanish to sink their treasure fleet before the English had seized the ships. He knew the Queen would be more displeased with that than anything, even the fact that against her wishes all the trophies of war had been disembursed between the gentlemen adventurers and the mariners.

Ralegh himself grumbled that he had got little profit from the venture, save a lame leg which would be a reminder of Cadiz to the last day of his life. However, both he and Arthur had brought presents for their wives and children, though, as Bess told him as she clung to him in the first joy of reunion, his own presence was the greatest gift she could ask for.

'It might well have been all you'd have got if it had been left to Essex,' Ralegh told the two women. 'He made sure the best and first choice of the booty went to the soldiers, and left us mariners to fend for ourselves.'

But it was enough for Bess to have her Walter back, though she shuddered over his wounded leg. It was torn with shell-splinters and didn't seem to be healing the way his other wounds had done.

For Wat, his father's return was heaven. Crowing with delight, he sat on Sir Walter's broad shoulders and beat a tattoo with his small hard fists on the curly black hair.

The Raleghs, with Arthur and Anna, went on a visit to Knole, where the venture was discussed and the battle refought. They enjoyed their stay but, as Bess said when they left, it was good to be riding in the direction of Sherborne once more. She had suggested Sir Walter ride in a coach because of his wound, but he viewed the suggestion with scorn.

'I wonder why the common people – aye, and others too – are so taken in by Essex?' mused Bess as they rode beside each other through the summer heat.

'Oh, because he's got the amazing beauty of a young Knight of King Arthur's Court.

132

He always appears the height of chivalry and graciousness to the poor. He has the same gift for wooing a multitude that the Queen has, only he has youth and beauty on his side as well, whereas she has to rely more now on her powerful personality.'

'But the men who serve under him – he does little for them yet they sing his praises,' objected Bess.

'They admire his dashing courage, even when it's their own lives he's so prodigal with,' returned Ralegh a trifle bitterly. He had told Bess of the taking of Cadiz so nearly ruined by the heavy loss of life, through Essex trying to land men in small boats which had overturned in the choppy seas, drowning many.

Ralegh himself knew the love of his men, for his mariners had followed him willingly to Guiana and hundreds of miles up the unknown dangerous river Orinoco. In his own West Country the common people turned out to cheer him. But unlike Essex, he could put forth no show for the populace. He could be unwittingly tactless in situations requiring the utmost care. Though on occasion he lied without a thought, on another occasion he would speak the truth which the rest of the company wished to keep hidden. Bess, looking at his profile, sighed and smiled at herself for sighing.

As Sherborne drew nearer, Walter became

lost in a dream. Bess felt a little inner pang that she scarcely acknowledged, even to herself. In body he rode beside her, his little son on the saddle before him, but in spirit he was far away, scheming to return to the tormented worship of 'That most chaste and fair Diana', who ruled England, and who ruled the men of England. She had loved Sir Walter once, and might do so again.

But the Queen, thought Bess, will hate me for the rest of her life.

EIGHT

RETURN TO FAVOUR

It was just after Christmas, in early January 1597. The Ralegh family were sitting round the fire whilst Bess tried to teach Wat to make a cat's cradle with string, and Sir Walter read a book.

A knock on the door disturbed the quiet scene. Peter Venn entered, bursting with importance.

'A messenger, Sir Walter,' he said somewhat breathlessly, 'straight come from London he have! He's got a letter for you. Can I take him to the kitchen to rest and warm himself before setting out on his return journey? It's mortal cold out.'

Sir Walter held out his hand for the letter and Peter Venn handed it over reluctantly. He would have dearly liked to know the contents, but since he couldn't read he had been unable even to peep to any profit.

'Certainly, Peter.' He scanned the letter swiftly. 'Tell the poor fellow we'll find him a bed and a meal tonight. The weather is not fit for a long ride.'

Peter, tugging his forelock, backed out of the room still staring curiously at the letter, and Bess sighed thankfully as the shutting of the door stopped the draught which had whistled amongst the rushes and chilled her to the bone.

Walter perused the letter in silence made somehow greater by the wind which howled round the house and the sleet which bounced down the chimney and hissed as it hit the fire. Wat raised his head to speak, but Bess motioned him to be quiet. There was something in her husband's face that she found difficult to read. The letter was of some importance obviously. Was it the longed-for summons back to Court? But his face showed no elation, only a growing pain.

'What is it, dear heart?' Bess asked at last, unable to bear the uneasy silence any longer.

Ralegh got up and knelt beside her, his arm round her shoulders.

'The letter is from Robert Cecil, my bird. He tells us–' He paused, tightening his grip round Bess. 'My heart, Elizabeth Cecil is dead. Cecil is numbed with grief. He swears he will think no more of marriage for he could meet no other lady to rival his wife.'

Bess raised her eyes to Sir Walter's face. Tears glistened, but did not fall.

'Poor Elizabeth. They'd been married scarcely seven years. And now Robert will be left to care alone for young Will and the girls. Walter, Will Cecil is such a weakly, sick child. He needs a mother's care and love to fill out his cheeks with health and stop him pining. Perhaps Robert will let him spend some time here with us at Sherborne. The company of another lad would be good for Wat, too – there's only a couple of years difference in their ages.'

'It's good of you to think of the boy, for I know how deeply you must grieve for the loss of Elizabeth's friendship,' said Ralegh, getting to his feet. 'I must write to Cecil now, telling him how truly we feel for him.'

'Yes, I'll write too. I'll suggest he sends Will to us for the summer, shall I?' asked Bess eagerly. 'The messenger can take both letters back with him when he returns to London tomorrow. We'll give him money, of course.'

Ralegh, on his way to the door, nodded absently. 'Yes, the messenger shall take our letters,' he murmured, then paused, un-decided. 'I have it in mind to go to Durham House for a while when the weather brightens,' he told her. 'Cecil mentions little but Elizabeth's untimely death, but he does say he longs for our company. You'll come with me and bring Wat?'

'For a while, perhaps,' agreed Bess.

So when the worst of the winter was over the Raleghs set out for Durham House. Ralegh was allowed back at Court but he did not take up again his former position of Captain of the Guard. However, Ralegh had his plans. He intended to bring about a reconciliation between Cecil and Essex, who hated each other so heartily. That, he knew, would please the Queen above all things. However, it was a difficult task. The Earl despised Cecil as a clerk and Cecil had a morbid nervous fear that people knowing they were the same age might compare unfavourably his slight, crooked figure and nervous, sensitive face with the tall, beautiful frame of England's Sir Lancelot.

Bess, for her part, would have liked to see Cecil married again, but she perceived how losing Elizabeth had hardened him against the possibility of re-marriage, and didn't attempt to introduce him to any ladies hunting for husbands.

She felt less enmity to Essex now than ever before. At Cadiz, Walter had told her how they had dined aboard each other's flagships and had in those brief meetings found that neither was quite the villain the other had imagined. Besides, despite the Queen's displeasure, he had knighted over sixty men at Cadiz and one of them had been her brother, now Sir Arthur Throckmorton.

On day in April Ralegh entered the house

much elated, with a spring in his step despite his limp.

'Bess,' he called, 'set out my best attire, my bird! The impossible is achieved! Tonight Essex has invited Cecil and myself to dine at Essex House. Now they can be friends and the Queen can have some peace at last.'

'Some piece of Sir Walter?' quipped Bess slyly, standing on tiptoe to kiss him. Sir Walter grinned and admitted, 'Well, we are going to discuss a plan to attack the Spanish treasure fleet off the Azores. If we win great fortune, I am sure to get back my post as Captain of the Guard. Besides, money is always useful.'

'Oh, always,' mocked Bess, looking around her at the rich tapestries and furnishings that filled their town house. 'For we are so much in need of every groat we can scrape together, are we not?'

'Don't laugh at me, woman, I'm determined to bring this reconciliation about, or it's no Islands voyage for me,' said Walter, smiling down at the impish face turned up to his.

Bess hurried away to lay out clean linen and all Sir Walter's finest array, and when he returned home that night, very late and more than a little drunk, she sat up in bed and said impatiently, 'Well?'

'Well indeed,' said Ralegh a trifle thickly, slipping on the rushes and throwing his best doublet in an untidy heap on the clothes chest. 'We are friends, Bess. Why, we are as good as at sea already, that I'll swear. Old Burghley has given almost all his res – res – reshponshibility to Robert, and he'll push it through with her Grace.'

'Come to bed, you malt-worm,' giggled Bess.

'Are you inshin – siner – oh hang it, are you saying I'm drunk?'

'Well, pot-valiant,' conceded Bess, pulling Sir Walter on to the bed and tenderly tucking the sheets round him.

'I hate a drunkard, and no man of Devon is affected by a few cups of wine,' protested Ralegh sleepily. 'Besides, it was in a good cause. I tell you, I'm as good as back in favour, my bird.'

Bess, knowing well Sir Walter's dislike of drunkenness, forebore to tease him further but, getting into bed, snuggled close to his already sleeping body. 'I won't think of his Islands voyage tonight,' she murmured. 'I'll pretend we are going to spend the summer at dear Sherborne, just the three of us together, in quiet happiness and content.'

Walter gave an uneasy moan and turned to face her, breathing wine fumes into her face so that Bess was once again overtaken by giggles.

'By morning I'll be drunk myself, without ever having taken so much as a sip of wine,' she told her sleeping husband. 'And if you have a collossal headache in the morning, you'll never admit it, because Devon men are hard-headed, capable of drinking every other man under the table and never even growing blurred in their speech.'

As she turned away from the fumes of the wine she thought uneasily how seldom her husband drank other than sparingly. It must indeed have been an important matter for him to have allowed himself to drink enough to arrive back at Durham House at three in the morning lurching despite the aid of his stick.

Then she banished thoughts from her mind and sank speedily into a deep sleep.

As Ralegh had foretold, the evening spent at Essex House did indeed seem to turn his fortunes. Once more, Ralegh was allowed into the Queen's presence and became increasingly aware of how Essex had usurped his place at her side. But he did not mind as he would once have done.

He would always love and honour his Queen as a supreme ruler and brilliant woman, but he would never again muddle in his own mind this love with what he now had – the true love between a man and his beloved wife. Elizabeth may have sensed this. If so, she didn't appear to resent it. She joined in the talks with Essex and Ralegh and, of course, her chief advisor, Cecil, with only tepid enthusiasm.

No one could have told what would have happened to the longed-for voyage if Spain hadn't suddenly sent a second armada against England. Even when this was dispersed once again by the weather, the three eager men managed to persuade the Queen that their best course was to try to finish off the remains of the Spanish fleet which had taken refuge in Ferrol. Then, they said, they would sail on to intercept the Spanish treasure fleet.

'Sir Walter is managing his part in the preparations so well that the Queen has given him full authority to take his place as Captain of the Guard,' Bess told Anna joyfully. 'Of course, I know I must be without him again for many months, but if he does well on this venture it will bring him great happiness.'

'Who is in command?' asked Anna without much real curiosity.

Bess flushed slightly. 'The Earl of Essex,' she said shortly. 'Pray heaven he doesn't get too full of his own importance and imperil the success of the voyage.'

'When the fleet sails, will you come and visit us at Paulerspury?' enquired Anna kindly. 'You know how Arthur and I enjoy your company, and little Wat is always welcome.'

Remembering Wat's raid on his aunt's

stillroom, Bess had to suppress a smile.

'No, my dear, though it's kind of you to ask us. We'll spend the time at Sherborne. Someone must look after it and, so far, the summer has not been a good one. I may not be of much practical use, but at least in Sir Walter's absence I can tell the servants yes or no when they ask. With no one down at the estate to turn to, they are apt to act not at all rather than risk a false move.'

Bess was certainly right about the bad summer. Never, it seemed, had it rained and stormed so constantly. The economic distress and consequent famine made Bess glad to be on her own estates doing the best for her own people, and when the fleet had to put back to port because of the weather, Sir Walter made a flying visit to his Bess at Sherborne.

He told her that things were being made difficult between himself and Essex mainly by the implacable hatred borne against him by Sir Christopher Blount, Essex's great friend and also his latest stepfather. Lettice's third husband was an unpleasant young man. Many said he had been her lover during Leicester's lifetime, but Ralegh dismissed this as he said Sir Christopher could scarcely have been out of leading strings. Smiling a sardonic farewell as he rode off to rejoin his ships, Walter called softly down to Bess, 'We both be cradle-snatchers, Lettice and I, but I believe she catches them even younger than I do.'

Smiling, Bess had to admit that Lettice Knollys deserved the nickname of 'The She-Wolf' bestowed on her by the Queen, for her appetite for men was endless.

Bess and Wat spent rather a dull summer down at Sherborne, only enlivened by Robert Cecil, who brought young Will down to stay with them, and spent some ten days there himself, watching the two little boys play together. He advised Bess on the management of the estate and how the drainage system should be laid to best advantage in the new cherry orchard. When he and Bess sat alone in the evenings his eyes rested with gentle melancholy on her golden head bent over her stitchery, whilst her skin glowed rose in the firelight, and envy of Ralegh ate into his heart.

Sometimes it seemed to Bess, going up to her great lonely bedchamber, that she was only half alive when Sir Walter was away. She walked, talked, ate, played with the children. But inside her the small secret chamber of her personality known only to herself and her lover was empty. Numb and waiting, waiting for his return.

She didn't tell Ralegh this of course. She was far too fond a wife. She wrote cheerful letters to him and to Cecil, telling them how the boys were thriving despite the dreadful weather, which quite put at end to outdoor sports.

Wat was quick and clever for his age and though not quite four he played checkers with Bess and sometimes even beat her, crowing with delight. Little Will, watching enviously, soon got the idea. Though older than Wat his schooling had been neglected because of his constant ill-health. Now, fitter and happier than he had been for months, his intellectual capacity began to show itself.

Wat was still not breeched and very much resented this whenever it entered his head to think about his petticoats. He tore them whenever possible, kept them constantly dirty, and refused to wear the little lace cap on his curls.

On one point, however, Bess remained firm. Wat should be breeched only when his father was home to take part in the simple ceremony of making a little boy out of a baby.

So when Bess hired a tutor for the two boys she chose a gentle, understanding young man. He was told the story of the despised petticoats and Will's ill-health and promised neither boy should be pushed in his work. So in an age where knowledge was crammed compulsorily into the very young, both boys blossomed into a natural love of learning. Their minds were not similar, but they both rejoiced in acquiring knowledge.

Ralegh's return from the Islands voyage was a mixed blessing. Bess was dismayed to hear how badly Essex had mismanaged the voyage. Ralegh told her in confidence that there had been times when he had entertained doubts of the Earl's complete sanity. 'His greed for power is too strong for a normal emotion,' he confessed to Bess uneasily.

Bess, for her part, cried in secret over the clothes riddled with bullet holes which her husband had worn when he and his men stormed Fayal, the only successful part of the venture.

Ralegh, on the other hand, began to look like a cat that's been at the cream. Essex didn't like the Queen's somewhat cool reception of him when he returned to Court and showed it by being as rude as he knew how – and Essex could excel at being rude.

It ended violently when he deliberately turned his back on the Queen in a fit of pique. Elizabeth, as quick to anger and as careful of her due as ever a monarch could be, boxed his ears. Essex, every proud nerve on end, flung himself from Court into voluntary retirement.

Ralegh stepped easily into the breach. Now he was older, a man with a wife and family. He was more restful, less demanding than the Ralegh Elizabeth had known, infinitely more restful than Essex. His relationship with the Queen was no longer that pretence of devoted lover and disdainful maid that had been so difficult to maintain earlier in their lives. Now she used Sir Walter as an ambassador for his country, knowing how pleasant he could make himself to those envoys of foreign powers who visited her Court.

Bess spent quite a lot of time with Ralegh at Durham House. There, at last, little Wat had his wish. One day the tailor delivered his first suit of real boy's clothes, a doublet of scarlet velvet slashed with yellow taffeta showing bombasted trunk hose which were full and padded and came just above his knees, and light grey stockings with yellow and red sash garters. A small white ruff at the neck, soft red velvet pumps on his feet, a narrow-brimmed cap trimmed with a feather and a little dagger completed his boy's attire.

'How tall he looks,' said Bess, with tears of pride in her eyes. 'How well the suit becomes him. Now do you feel yourself a man, Wat?'

'I'm a man like father,' Wat boasted, strutting up and down the hall like a peacock whilst the servants admired and his parents beamed. 'When I'm old enough I'll go to sea like father does, and chase the Spaniards.'

'He's a chip off the old block,' friends said

when they saw Wat dressed in his grand new clothes. Many friends now came to Durham House to see Bess, for she would never be allowed back to the Court. They found her very little changed. She still retained her looks and her vitality and natural charm were never to desert her.

Now positions were reversed. It was Arthur who came to London and stayed at Durham House with Bess, instead of the Raleghs coming up from the country to stay at Mile End. Arthur and Bess went to see a performance of the play *Richard II* put on at the Globe Theatre by the Lord Chamberlain's men and afterwards listened to the gossip of other play-goers.

'Surely, 'tis plainly enough shown that our young Earl plans to overthrow her Grace,' whispered one homely farmer up for a week's visit, to his friend. 'Why, you told me yourself that the Lord Chamberlain's men have the Earl of Southampton for patron, and he is a close friend of the Earl of Essex.'

'Hush, will you?' growled his companion. 'Our Essex wouldn't harm the Queen. But he's not at Court at the moment. They say that Ralegh has usurped his place.' He spat his disgust into the gutter and Bess, flinching, pulled Arthur away.

'The common people hate Sir Walter. They blame him for Essex's disgrace, which is of his own making. Sometimes I fear for him,' Bess told Arthur when they had reached the safety of Durham House.

'Don't worry, Bess,' consoled Arthur. 'The people can't help but be pleased by Essex. I was very taken with him myself before I got to know his uncertain temper. He's all youth and charm, courage and gaiety. Sir Walter doesn't usurp his place either at Court or in the Queen's affections. She loves Essex as she loves her lost youth. Sir Walter is young at heart, but he has forty-five years of living behind him. He doesn't make the Queen imagine herself a girl again.'

'Unfortunately, the people don't stop to consider things like that,' Bess said bitterly. 'They see only two things – Essex is at Court, Ralegh out of favour. Then behold, Ralegh is back in favour with the Queen, and Essex sulks at Wanstead. So they put their own simple construction on it, and my poor Walter takes the blame.'

'Come, don't take it all so seriously. I wish I hadn't taken you to see the play,' said Arthur uneasily. 'What of the summer? You won't remain in London at risk of the plague? Will you go to Sherborne, or can I persuade you to bring the boys – for I naturally include Will Cecil as well as Wat – down to Paulerspury?'

'It's kind of you, Arthur, and I'd welcome it in many ways, but we shall go down to Sherborne,' said Bess a trifle listlessly.

'Weymouth is near and the boys are keen sea-bathers and love the beach. Then there is always the chance that Sir Walter may be able to come to us there for a few weeks and take the waters at Bath for his leg.'

So when summer came she and the boys went down to Sherborne. They stayed there a while, enjoying the soft fruit season and the milder weather which seemed to have succeeded the three terrible summers. Then they went down to Weymouth where Sir Walter joined them and proved as great a success as always with the boys, who adored him.

Bess came to them on the beach one morning from their lodgings. Sir Walter was building a small model of Guiana on the sands and showing the boys how the great river Orinoco had overflowed its banks and flooded the jungle for many miles, forcing them to turn back.

The boys were aiding the spreading of the seawater flood with their spades, widening and deepening the channel with concentrated pleasure, as Sir Walter bade them.

'My dearest, there is a letter come from John Mere, the man you left in charge of the work and improvements at Sherborne. He says the river is about to be turned from its course to run through our grounds and feels you might like to be present on such an occasion.'

The little boys cried out with glee and Walter got to his feet, brushing sand off his hose with one hand and holding out the other for the letter.

'Yes, yes, he's right. A sight I'd not miss for a small fortune. Nor shall the boys miss it. We'll go back to Sherborne tomorrow.'

'But you intended going to Bath and then to London. Won't you be missed at Court?' ventured Bess.

Ralegh gave a sarcastic snort. 'It grows dull at Court. The Queen is absent-minded, disinterested. Worrying only about what troubles may have befallen her beloved Robert Devereux. Yet she does not forget to throw constant work at my head so that I am for ever bear-leading some foreign dignitary around London. Sometimes I scarcely know whether my native tongue is French, Spanish, Italian or English.'

'Ah yes, as you say, my love,' murmured Bess wickedly as they left the beach, 'I suppose it's through your work, for I've heard it said that Sir Walter Ralegh speaks all tongues admirably, excepting only English.'

They laughed together whilst the boys frolicked on ahead. Ralegh's deep Devonshire burr would never change now. Young Wat copied it, and so did Will Cecil when his father was not within hearing. To Bess it was the dearest sound in the world, showing how little in actual fact wealth and an important position had changed Sir Walter.

The return to Sherborne was in the nature of a triumph. Everyone on the estate was glad to have them back and especially glad to see Sir Walter, the master they admired so much but saw so little. Even Smith, the cook, said that it was against nature for one of his calling to prepare meals only for the other servants.

The boys and Walter spent most of their time out of doors watching the mighty digging and labouring that went on to divert the river from its natural course, so that it might flow through the grounds of Sherborne and beautify the estate still further.

The day came when the work was completed and the dark brown flood poured into its new bed.

'It looks rather horrible at the moment,' Sir Walter admitted to Bess as they stood looking down on the yellow foam that swirled and sucked against the earth banks. 'But wait until the water has had a chance to settle and make itself a permanent bed. Waterweeds will flourish, we'll plant water-lilies and I'll introduce fish into our part of the river. Why, we'll even have some duck and maybe a pair of swans.'

'Why haven't we peacocks? I'd dearly love to see peacocks strutting on our lawns,' shouted Wat above the gurgle of the river.

His father turned to him indulgently. 'So

you shall, Wat, so you shall. But first things first. In a day or two, when the water is clear and sparkling again, I'll bring some swans.'

Those swans were to prove the first real sign of animosity between father and son. They had been installed several days and were to be seen complacently cruising up and down their favourite strip of the river. Bess and Sir Walter were sitting once more in the shade of the cedar tree. It was a hot day. Sir Walter was smoking his pipe to keep off the midges, he said, and Bess was laboriously mending a pair of Wat's torn hose. A sudden shout from the direction of their new river made them look up.

'Wat! He's fallen in!' said Bess, pale to the lips. She and Sir Walter ran across the intervening gardens and walks with Walter vainly reminding Bess that their son swam like a fish. When they reached the river bank the sight that met their eyes was quite unexpected.

On the green grass beside the idling water lay stretched out the body of a swan. Its eyes were closed, its beak a-gape. A short distance away the bird's mate stood, wings outstretched like a bird of heraldry, uttering short menacing hisses.

Beside the swan knelt the two boys. Wat was laughing and smacking the swan on the back, Will seemed to be anxiously trying to massage some life into its thickly plumaged body.

'How came this swan by its downfall?' asked Sir Walter quietly.

The two boys looked up, both flushing scarlet. Wat, speechless but still grinning from ear to ear, held up the offending catapult.

'Why did you shoot at it, Wat? Did the swan attack you?' asked Bess helplessly. She could see from Sir Walter's face that he was seriously annoyed.

'No, he didn't attack us. Me and Will were taking turns hitting the old target with the catapult, only it was difficult to tell when we'd got a bull, because pebbles aren't like arrows, they don't stay in the target. Then the swans came gliding by and I thought if I hit one it would fall over and that would prove how good a shot I am.' Wat paused, breathless after his long speech. 'And it got on to the bank because we threw it bread, and I fired at it, and it fell over,' he ended, still looking pleased with himself.

Will, seeing the angry look on Sir Walter's face, said hastily, 'No harm done, Sir. Look, the swan is beginning to stir.'

'You hurt the poor bird, Wat,' Bess said gently as the bird got dizzily to its feet and began waddling in a drunken fashion towards its mate. 'Are you sorry you hurt the swan?'

But Wat wasn't attending. 'Look at it,

tacking like a Spanish galleon,' he shouted. 'Shall I whack its arse with another pebble, Will?'

Ralegh, thoroughly annoyed by the whole affair and outraged by Wat's last remark, seized his offspring and administered a hard spanking, the first Wat had ever received in all his short life. The loud roars this brought forth sounded more like temper than pain and indeed the scarlet of his face seemed to indicate that he was surprised and outraged more than hurt.

He didn't take his punishment lying down either, wriggling, biting and kicking all the while, so that Ralegh was glad enough to stand him down after half a dozen whacks, saying sternly, 'You will not fire your catapult at the swans or any of the livestock. Understand me, Wat?'

Wat, backing away with one hand on the seat of his small breeches, said in a mutter, 'It's *my* catapult. When you're dead they'll be *my* swans. I'll fire where I choose.' He turned to make off but Bess grabbed him as he tried to pass her and Ralegh took the catapult, broke it across his knee and threw the pieces in the river.

'You beast, oh, you beast!' shouted Wat. Hurling himself at his father he began raining blows on him with small hard fists.

Ralegh, his temper really aroused, pinioned his son's arms and was about to continue with the spanking when Bess intervened.

'Please don't hit him, dear heart,' she begged. 'It's my fault, too, you know. He's been over-indulged, and he's got your temper and mine too, alas.'

She turned to Wat, who still showed signs of nothing but extreme fury.

'You love me, don't you, my lamb?'

Wat nodded, the colour beginning to fade from his face and his eyes losing their hot look.

'Then for my sake tell your father you're truly sorry and won't hurt the livestock again.'

Wat gave an impatient sigh. 'I'm truly sorry and won't hurt the livestock again,' he said in a rush. Then his sense of humour coming to the fore, he added, 'Father, the swan *did* look funny, didn't it? Just how you described the Spanish galleons with their sails all spread trying to tack up the Channel before the wind, with our fleet hot on their tails.'

Ralegh released his small prisoner and laughed reluctantly. 'Aye, you've got a point,' he admitted. 'But no more devilry, mind. You've inherited my quick temper and love of mischief. They've done me no good and they'll do you none. Go to the stable, both of you. Your ponies have been idle long enough.'

All else forgotten, the boys rushed out of

sight. But Ralegh couldn't forget the little incident. It seemed to show that the boy had inherited more than his father's looks and his mother's charm. He had inherited the Ralegh strong will and quick temper along with some sort of rebelliousness against authority all his own. This, Sir Walter knew, was no good thing.

'We must curb that temper, it could lead to his downfall,' he told Bess.

NINE

THE FALL OF ESSEX

'They say, mistress, that the Queen means James of Scotland to be her heir, but won't name him outright because it would be signing her death warrant,' ventured Myers as she helped Lady Ralegh scatter the new rushes on the floor of the main bedchamber at Sherborne.

'I daresay it's true, Myers,' said Bess, pushing her hair off her damp forehead and picking up an armful of fresh rushes from the pile by the door. 'Truth to tell, all the world wants a Protestant ruler. No one fancies another Civil War or being ruled by Rome again.'

'Who does Sir Walter prefer?' asked Myers slyly. But Bess just shrugged and smiled. 'He would like the Queen's Grace to rule for ever,' she replied with more honesty than she realised.

Everyone else was looking to the future. Elizabeth was not, after all, immortal. Cecil was in correspondence with James and had promised his allegiance when Elizabeth died. He declared he would have horsemen posted along the route to Scotland so that the tidings of her death would reach James without delay. Even Essex had looked far enough ahead to write to James, assuring him of his devotion when he came to England as its next ruler.

Everyone who had a place at Court and wanted to keep it got in touch with James. 'In case,' they would have explained obscurely.

Everyone, that is, except Ralegh. Bess knew he would take no steps in that direction. He had nothing against James, but whilst Elizabeth lived she was Queen and one did not look beyond that.

So life continued fairly quietly for the Raleghs. Essex got his way once more with the Queen and was given an enormous army to go to Ireland and suppress the rebel, Tyrone. But he allowed himself to be swayed by the plausible tongues of the Irish into marching around the countryside putting down small rebellions, whilst Tyrone chuckled to himself in safety and watched this proud, foolish Englishman lose his army to guerrilla fighters, disease, and desertion.

The Queen wrote a sarcastic letter to Essex, telling him she was apparently paying for him to go on a Progress but that he was not to return without her express orders. Essex, frightened by Tyrone, frightened for the first time by the realisation that he was not capable of carrying out the task in hand, was not frightened enough of Elizabeth.

'Essex has returned from Ireland against the Queen's command,' Ralegh told his wife one evening.

'What happened? Was she very annoyed?' asked Bess curiously.

'He burst into her withdrawing chambers. She was doing her hair.'

Bess gasped. She knew her mistress well enough to realise how this must have infuriated and discomposed her. To be caught unpainted, unready, could only have served to add fuel to the fire of her slowly kindling wrath.

'I feel sorry for Essex,' she said slowly, remembering how cruel Elizabeth's tongue could be when she felt inclined.

'No need. She laughed it off, I'm told. He's confined to his room for the moment, but that's all. You know the Queen, my bird. She'll want time – lots of it – to think this one out before she acts.'

But for once Ralegh had underestimated Elizabeth. What followed, followed swiftly. Essex was released and his command in Ireland given into other hands. He himself was kept from the Court.

'Where will that lead? Poor Frances, what a husband she has,' sighed Bess.

'Lead? Why, if Robert Devereux keeps his head, it'll lead nowhere. The people sing songs and ballads of their noble young Earl of Essex. Elizabeth both loves and hates him. But she has nothing but love for her people – and wants nothing but love from them. If Essex only behaves sensibly for once, all will go well.'

And indeed for a time all went well. Later in the year the Queen appointed Ralegh Governor of Jersey. The Raleghs, accompanied by young Will Cecil of course, went as far as Weymouth together. Then Sir Walter took ship for his new appointment, leaving Bess and the boys to the joys of sea-bathing and the beach.

They had a slight shock whilst they were enjoying their usual summer routine at Weymouth, for Bess received a letter telling her there had been a fire at Durham House. Fortunately it wasn't serious, but Bess seized the opportunity of writing to Cecil, ostensibly telling him that the fire had been started by a servant of the Darcys' who lodged in the lower part of the house. Really, it was to suggest that since her husband had spent so much money on the house it might be given to them outright instead of being a gift at the Queen's pleasure. Bess thought defiantly that she had a right to think of such things even if her husband would not.

Cecil, when he read the letter, laughed to himself. If James became King and the Raleghs owned Durham House, he could not take it from them. As things stood, he could repossess it as soon as he was crowned. Bess wasn't worrying about Sherborne because that had been made safe by a deed of gift signed by Ralegh, giving it to young Wat.

Cecil wondered as he perused the letter, so typical of lively, intelligent Bess, whether the Raleghs realised the devious game he himself was playing. Slowly but surely he was poisoning the King of Scots mind against Sir Walter. By the time Elizabeth died, he reasoned, the King would fall into his hand like a ripe apple. He would bring his Scottish favourites to Court with him, and he would have scant time for Ralegh, whom he already believed to be an atheist and a man who loved war. James was a coward who feared war desperately for his own sake, not as Elizabeth did, for her country's sake.

The next time Cecil visited Sherborne to see how Will went on, he wondered uneasily as he rode up to the great front door what his reception would be. Surely Bess and Walter could not be so blind that they realised nothing of his devious plotting.

Apparently they could. His welcome was as warm as ever. When Cecil left he felt he could continue his double game in safety. Ralegh had assured him that though he had heard rumours of Cecil corresponding with James, he discounted them. Bess, smiling and pleasant, had reservations. She had seen the half-frightened look in his eyes when he entered the house. But she kept her fears to herself.

'Have you heard anything further from Jersey about your potato crops?' asked Bess one evening as she worked on the tapestry square on her lap.

'You'll never finish that tapestry if you keep laying it down to talk of potato crops,' teased Walter, knowing well his wife's secret aversion to needlework. 'Why, I'd be willing to take a bet that my potatoes will be flourishing all over Jersey before those chairs have seats.'

Bess picked up her needle with a martyred sigh and Walter continued, 'However, though it's too soon to know whether potatoes will do well in Jersey, they are certainly flourishing in Ireland. Essex was good enough to tell me that the last time I saw him.'

'This is the first Christmas we've had Will with us at Sherborne,' said Bess suddenly, tiring of potato talk. 'Do we have other visitors? I'd have liked Arthur and Anna to bring the girls down for the festive season, but Arthur is such a home-loving body. He's found himself a new doctor, too, so I don't suppose he'd be willing to leave Paulerspury.' She giggled, glancing at Sir Walter. 'My brother is three years younger than you, love, but to read his letters or hear him talk anyone would take him for an ailing sixty-year-old.'

'Come, don't laugh at your brother, you wicked wench. No, we have no other visitors staying with us this year. Cecil stays with his two daughters and his elder brother's family.'

So down at Sherborne, that Christmas of 1600 was pleasant indeed. Perhaps the last really restful and peaceful Christmas either the Raleghs or Queen Elizabeth were ever again to know.

In January, the Raleghs returned to Durham House. Sir Walter seemed to Bess to come home to her from the Queen more tired and irritable than had been his wont, but he said nothing to her of any particular worries at Court, and she knew better than to enquire.

Then, on Sunday, 8th February, Essex at last broke out. He attempted to take the city of London and to get the Queen at his mercy, no one seemed to quite know why. The people of London, in whom he placed implicit faith, failed him. No one rallied to his cry that he was protecting the Queen against her enemies, and he ended this time really imprisoned – in the Tower, for the Queen's patience was at an end.

Essex was tried for treason and in his desperate attempts to save himself he was willing to sacrifice anything, the best of his friends, his beloved elder sister Penelope, even his mother. He blamed them all, saying they had conceived the notion and he had but carried it out. He cried aloud that his sister, married to Lord Rich, was also the mistress of Lord Mountjoy, and even his dearest friends doubted his sanity.

'Nothing will save him now,' Ralegh told Bess a trifle sadly when he got home after the trial. 'The Queen has tired of his perpetual sulking and trouble-making. And if you ask me, he signed his own death warrant when he last quarrelled with her.'

'Why? Whatever did he say?' asked Bess, astonished. Elizabeth had borne so many insults from Essex, even to being called 'A King in petticoats'.

'He said to her "You are cankered, and your condition is as crooked as your carcass",' replied Ralegh reluctantly. 'Mind you, I've no doubt the words were uttered in a heat of rage, for lately Essex has scarcely been responsible for his actions, let alone his speech.'

'What a cruel thing for him to say,'

interjected Bess indignantly. 'I suppose he referred to the fact that she holds one shoulder high. Oh, how could he hurt her so, after all she's done for him?'

Ralegh gazed at Bess reproachfully. 'Carries one shoulder high? The Queen? No, my bird, you must be imagining it.'

Bess marvelled at the blindness of this man she loved so well. There wasn't a maid of honour at Court, nor a lady in waiting, no not even a tiring woman, who didn't know that much of the Queen. But apparently men saw her as she wanted them to see her – straight and slim, proud and elegant.

All but Essex. He, the darling of her last years, saw her only as a provider. His contemptuous eye had noticed her physical defect, and now his remark – and of course his treasonable actions – would lead him to the scaffold.

No time was wasted. The love of the mob for their hero had risen up, so Essex and five of his fellow conspirators were beheaded. To everyone's surprise the Earl of Southampton, who had been prominent in the uprising even to the extent of getting his friend amongst the Chamberlain's men to present the play *Richard II* at the Globe just before the rebellion, was not amongst the men who paid the final penalty.

Elizabeth had always hated violence. Throughout her long reign she had tried to keep the peace between Catholic and Protestant subjects without resorting to the death penalty, preferring rather to demand fines and smaller punishments. Now she was glad to be able to have put down a dangerous conspiracy with the death of only six men.

'I even feel sorry for that – that She-Wolf today,' Bess sobbed out to Ralegh when the executions were over and she was packing to leave for Sherborne. 'She's outlived her son, the apple of her eye, and seen that son bring about the death of her third husband and try to blame her for his doings. She has even had the shame of her daughter made public by that same son. Oh, I know they say she's been a wicked woman in her time, with men as lovers whenever one of her husbands turned his back, but I think today she has been paid back twofold for whatever evil she may have done.'

'Aye, Sir Christopher Blount also paid the price for loving Essex,' admitted Ralegh. 'But dry your eyes, my pretty one, the carriage with your luggage is at the door, and the groom is holding your horse ready for you to ride to Sherborne, and some peace and quiet.'

Bess and the boys had been hurriedly despatched to Sherborne because Ralegh knew the fall of Essex would be laid at his door, though he had been completely blameless in the matter. In his office of Captain of the Guard he had to be present at the executions, but in order not to appear to gloat he had left the scaffold when Essex appeared, and watched the flash of the axe from a window of the Armoury in the Tower. To his grief he was told afterwards that Essex had asked to see him in his last moments, to beg his pardon for quarrels long past.

But none of this was heeded by the people. Elizabeth had forbidden the public performance of *Richard II* in the theatres, but she was powerless to stop street players from performing it, or singing songs in praise of Essex.

'Sweet England's pride is gone,
Welladay, Welladay!
Brave honour graced him still,
Gallantly, gallantly.

He ne'er did deed of ill,
Well it is known.
But envy, that foul fiend
Whose malice ne'er did end
Hath brought true virtue's friend
Unto his thrall.'

Thus sang the townspeople, and Sir Walter had sufficient sense to know that it was his own envy that was supposed to have brought about Essex's downfall.

But even safe in their beloved Sherborne, Bess heard the rumours about Ralegh and Cecil. She tried to shield the two boys from them, but they added to her fears for Walter.

'I wonder what the much-married Lettice will do now? Surely at her age she won't go hunting for a fourth husband?' Marjory asked idly when she came down to ease Bess's solitude, bringing her little daughter with her.

'Don't be unkind, Marjory,' protested Bess. 'She's lost everything. Oh, I know we used to laugh at her when we were foolish girls, but we're old enough now not to laugh at another's grief.'

'I didn't mean to laugh, I just can't imagine her without a man at her apron-strings,' said Marjory, flushing. 'How is Sir Walter managing to live with the slanders and lies that are hurled at his head whenever he walks the streets?'

'He is suffering, of course,' admitted Bess. 'Not only does he have the unjust anger of the crowds to deal with, but though several times his name has been put forward for a peerage, something – or someone – has always made sure it came to nought.'

'I know he has enemies,' agreed Marjory, 'but he will not attempt to conciliate them. He's older now, Bess. He's got you and Wat to consider. Couldn't he bend his stiff back for your sakes, if not his own?'

'We wouldn't ask it of him,' replied Bess promptly. 'But, anyway, he'll be down here with us soon to enjoy the summer months at Sherborne and Weymouth. He may go over to Jersey for a few weeks; he's very fond of the island,' she added.

'How the building goes on,' marvelled Marjory, looking about her. 'They all say "Sir Walter doth toil terribly".'

'Oh, he's a worker,' agreed Bess. 'He's never content unless he's supervising building or alterations. He gives advice to the tin miners in Cornwall, rushes hither and thither in London showing the foreign ambassadors the sights. His energy would be remarkable in a boy of twenty. At his age it's little short of miraculous.'

'And the Queen? How does she bear with the crowd's coolness towards her, and the nobles even? I'm told they are less quick to shout "God Save the Queen" than ever before?' asked Marjory.

Bess shook her head sadly. 'The Queen is old, Marjory, and she knows it. Essex made her know she was old. Ralegh says she doesn't even pretend any more. She rides, hunts, hawks – all as before, but the old sparkle is gone. The truth is she knows the people themselves are tired of being ruled by an old Queen. They want a King once more. Someone young and vigorous, as they imagine James to be.'

'Why should he not be young and vigorous? He's only a couple of years younger than you are, love,' teased Marjory.

'Oh, I've heard tales,' said Bess nonchalently. Lowering her voice she added, 'He likes young men – you know, Marjory, *likes* them, holds their hands in public and caresses them. He hates washing and rarely changes his linen. His legs are spindly and his eyes watery. He drinks. Ugh, imagine such a monarch after Elizabeth! I think the people will be sadly disappointed when James comes South.'

'Rumours can never be trusted,' protested Marjory. 'Nor can portraits – neither word-portraits nor those done in oils. Remember Henry VIII and Anne of Cleves? Now he was deceived by rumour and a portrait for one.'

'I wish these were just rumours,' said Bess darkly, 'for a man who likes pretty boys can never like Sir Walter, nor be liked by him. Now let's forget about intrigue and rumour, shall we? Let's go on the river. Would you like that, Rosy?'

The tiny dark-haired girl clinging to her mother's skirts nodded shyly but didn't remove her thumb from her mouth.

As they went towards the archery butts the two women talked of the difficulties of breaking a child of the habit of thumb sucking and the trials of curbing the high and wicked spirits of a spoilt only son. Affairs of State could be forgotten for a while, at least.

Time passed. Marjory and Rosamund left. Bess left the boys with their tutor at Sherborne and went to Durham House for a short stay. She returned precipitately.

Essex had been dead over a year, yet the crowd still sang for him. He was their golden boy, their blue-blooded martyr.

And as Essex, dead, was loved, so Ralegh and Cecil, alive, were hated. Bess thought with a little shudder of fear that no two men could ever have been so unpopular. Even the man in the street was aware now that Cecil was trafficking with the King of the Scots.

'Little Cecil tripping up and down:
He rules both Court and Crown',

they sang of him. And of Ralegh, worse. They forgot the taxes they didn't have to pay because Ralegh stood up for their rights in Parliament. They forgot he, too, had been poor once, like themselves. Roistering through the streets they sang openly:

'Ralegh doth time bestride:
He sits 'twixt wind and tide,

Yet uphill cannot ride
For all his bloody pride.

'He seeks taxes in the tin,
He polls the poor to the skin,
Yet he swears 'tis no sin—
Lord for thy pity!'

Bess was sickened by the songs, the crude jests, the whispers that lowered even the Queen, hinting that she was slow to name her successor because of a bastard son she had born by Seymour, or Leicester, or Hatton, or Essex, or (needless to say) Ralegh.

So Bess went back to Sherborne, to the comforting normality of her life there with the two boys. She was a very frightened woman. She had seen the Queen as she rode out and was shaken by the change in her. The white, unpainted face, the droop of that once upright body.

Ralegh frightened her more.

'She doesn't want to live,' he said despairingly. 'She knows the people are tiring of her and she has lived her life out for her people. Now she would die for them – and will, if I know my Queen. She is as set on death as others are on life.'

On the 24th March, 1603, Queen Elizabeth died. Her surgeons thought they could have saved her, but she would have none of them, turning her face to the wall and asking to be left to die in peace.

At the funeral Ralegh marched beside her coffin, a black plume in his helmet. It was his last duty to Elizabeth as Captain of her Guard. But it wasn't duty that forced the difficult tears from his eyes, blurring his vision and wrenching at his heart. This Queen that was more than an ordinary mortal was gone. What was he to do without her?

When he got back to Durham House after the funeral he shut himself up in his study in the turret overlooking the river and wrote, from his aching heart, more verses to her who was gone. He wrote of his thoughts of her as:

> '...A durable fire,
> In the mind ever burning,
> Never sick, never old, never dead,
> From itself never turning.'

As soon as he could, Ralegh rode down to Sherborne. Everyone knew that James was riding South – messengers had set out for Scotland as soon as the Queen was pronounced dead just as Cecil had promised. Bess would have liked to suggest that Sir Walter follow the lead of the rest of the Court and ride to meet James, but in the depth of his grief she wouldn't mention it. As usual, it was action that brought him back from morbid and painful thoughts. There was business to be seen to in the tin mines in Cornwall, and he set forth from Sherborne to forget his unhappiness in work.

It was from Cornwall that he rode to welcome the uncrowned King upon urgent representations from his friends to do so.

But Bess felt instinctively that a man of James' cut would look on her debonair, self-confident husband with less than liking, maybe even with envious hatred.

She remembered a chance remark of hers once to Sir Walter when she had first heard of James wearing bolstered garments to guard against assassination.

'He is bolstering his courage,' she had cried gaily. But now that nervous, padded little figure held the whip hand and it was herself who needed courage.

'Come into the garden with me, Wat,' she cried. 'It's spring and your father goes to welcome the new King. Let us pick some gillyflowers for the great hall.'

'Can I come too, Lady Bess?' called young Will Cecil. 'I've finished my lessons for today.'

Bess agreed gladly. Together they ran across the lawns to the beds where the gilly-flowers grew.

King James had come to them at the best time of the year, she told the boys. The beginning. 'He will be a young King of Spring,' she told them with breathless gaiety. 'He will welcome both your fathers to help him to rule his new kingdom.'

But the boys, echoing her laughter, eyed each other covertly. They had heard much talk of this James of Scotland, and he didn't sound like a King of Spring to them. More like a poor frightened spider of a King, who would need their fathers if he meant to keep his kingdom long.

Bess couldn't read their thoughts, but she could tell they were playing up to her mood, trying to give her mind the ease it sought.

Abruptly, she called for Peg to put the flowers in water and went up to her room with dragging footsteps. Once alone, she sat on the joint stool in front of the window and gazed unseeingly over the gardens.

This, then, was the end of an era.

But what, oh what, would the new reign bring?

TEN

THE TOWER GAPES

Within two months of the Queen's death, Bess's worst forbodings began to be fulfilled.

From Sherborne she got a letter from her husband, telling her how Durham House had been taken from him and restored to the Bishop of Durham.

'He has been given seventeen days to clear out all our possessions – seventeen days!' Bess complained passionately to Myers.

'Why, a commoner has a quarter's notice to quit before he can be put on the street,' exclaimed Myers indignantly.

'God alone knows what he will do with all his maps and books and all the furniture. Now Sir Walter will be forced to have a London lodging.'

Myers eyed her mistress with genuine distress. 'Would not the master be wiser to retire to his Irish estates perhaps?' she suggested. 'After all, he likes the Irish people well enough, and I'm sure most of us would follow him willingly if he chose to make Ireland his home.'

Bess sighed. 'Oh, Myers, you don't think it will come to that?'

The woman made no answer, but in the mirror their eyes met and Bess unwillingly acknowledged the truth her heart knew.

'If King James has taken Durham House, with so little notice, then he holds Sir Walter in distaste. You're right, of course, Myers. But we still have Sherborne. Surely the King cannot wrest that from us. Time enough to worry if he tries.'

Then in mid-July Bess received a letter from a friend. It was unsigned, merely telling her that Sir Walter had gone down to Windsor to attend the King on a hunting expedition. Whilst he waited for King James to appear, Robert Cecil had approached him and told him the Privy Council wanted speech with him. He was now, the anonymous writer continued, lodged in the Tower.

Bess, nearly demented with worry, rode post haste up to London, only to find she was refused permission to enter the Tower to see her husband.

Now indeed James began to show what he was made of. Troubles fell on the Raleghs thick and fast. Sir Walter had already been deprived of his London house and most of his important offices. Even the Wardenship of the Stanneries in Devon and Cornwall had been taken from him.

Now he lay in the Tower, whilst James' men haunted every part of the city, listening even to street gossip and tavern talkers to find evidence against Ralegh.

Bess, in growing fear, did not need to ask what the charge would be. Sir Walter had done no wrong, as he continually repeated. Therefore it would be a trumped-up charge of treason, punishable by death and an almost impossible crime of which to clear oneself.

Bess began to look wildly round her for someone she could trust, but before she could make a move she also was sent to the Tower. She left Wat in Marjory's care, with her promise to send him down to Beddington to her brother Nicholas if it became necessary.

Bess was now a prisoner in the Tower for the second time in her life. She was allowed to see no one, and she was refused permission to know whereabouts in the Tower Sir Walter was lodged. Myers shared her imprisonment and without her sensible, down-to-earth presence Bess sometimes felt she would have gone mad. It was not knowing anything for certain that drove her mind to fill with the wildest possibilities.

News filtered through to her when Sir Walter tried to commit suicide, but the attempt was unsuccessful. However, it threw the Tower into such an uproar that even Myers and Bess came to hear of it.

Crying silently into her pillow that night, Bess knew now what she had suspected. The charge would be treason and Sir Walter had so little hope of escaping sentence of guilty that he had tried suicide for her sake, and that of young Wat. Had the attempt been successful Bess would have been entitled to her one-third share of her husband's estates and would have held the rest in trust for Wat. But should Sir Walter die condemned of treason then the Crown took everything. She and Wat would be destitute, relying upon her brothers for their very bread.

Bess and Myers were released from the Tower just prior to the trial. They went at once to Marjory, who took them in.

The trial was, as it had to be, a farce. Sir Edward Coke was the chief prosecutor and treated Ralegh as though they were personal enemies. He attacked him with the foulest terms at his command, he abused and reviled him. Ralegh was not allowed to see his accuser and he conducted his own defence, which was made doubly difficult by the fact that no one seemed quite sure what the treasonable act was supposed to be. Nevertheless, Ralegh fought superbly. By all the laws of fairness and legality he should have been pronounced not guilty. But fairness and legality were not present at the trial. The judges were all his enemies – Robert Cecil was one of them – and the verdict was guilty. Ralegh was sentenced to be hanged, drawn and quartered.

Bess took the news with a calmness which Marjory found unnerving.

'He may have been found guilty,' she told Marjory quietly, 'yet it is said that before the trial all men believed in his guilt. Now there is scarcely a soul in England who would not swear he is innocent.'

'When does the sentence take place?' asked Marjory gently, taking her friend's cold hand and gently chaffing it between her own.

'On the thirteenth of December,' Bess answered dully. 'But Cecil swears that he shall have an honourable death – the axe – and not that put upon him by the court.'

'Bess, you must go to Paulerspury,' urged Marjory, 'or to Nicholas at Beddington. Nothing can now be gained but pain and distress by remaining in London. Sir Walter will go to Winchester until – until–'

'Until his death. You're right, Marjory. I can do no good here. But I'm poor company, and young Wat needs familiar faces round him. I'll take him down to Sherborne. There, at least for a while, we can forget the world and remember only past happiness.'

She went down to Sherborne and received a letter from Marjory telling her how three of the 'conspirators' had been reprieved on the very scaffold itself. But Marjory could hold out no hope of a similar reprieve for Sir Walter.

The last night had arrived. Ralegh's last night on earth. He had made his peace with God through the Bishop of Winchester. Now, alone in his room, he was writing. The last letter would be, of course, to Bess.

Alone, cold, his hand cramped, still he wrote on steadily, trying to give Bess comfort for the lonely years to come. He begged her to marry again, for the child's sake. He could give her no name of a friend to whom she might turn for help – his friends, it seemed, were there only to betray.

Ralegh stopped writing for a moment to think of Wat, so like himself. Quick-tempered, impetuous, spoilt. He added another line to his letter.

'Remember your poor child for his father's sake, that chose you and loved you in his happiest times.'

Steadily the pen scratched on. Finally he ended the letter. 'I can write no more. Time and death call me away.'

But the tired, ageing man did not stop writing. He turned, as was natural to him in distress, to poetry. In the cold hour before dawn he wrote what he felt of life and faith, when one was so soon to be snatched from him and the other put to the test.

'Give me my scallop shell of quiet,
My staff of faith to walk upon,
My scrip of joy, immortal diet,
My bottle of salvation,
My gown of glory, hope's true gage;
And thus I'll take my pilgrimage.

Blood must be my body's balmer;
No other balm will there be given.
Whilst my soul, like quiet palmer,
Travelleth towards the land of heaven.'

Still he wrote on, the poetry coming easily into his exhausted mind, until the first grey light of dawn began to steal through his windows. Yet when at last they came for him it was to tell him that his life was reprieved but that he was condemned to the Tower.

Housed once more in the Tower, he suffered a sort of delayed shock, combined with exhaustion. He learned from letters secretly passed to him that Cecil was helping Bess to claim as much as was possible so that she and Wat would not be condemned to utter poverty.

Bess saw all was right at Sherborne, then she sped to the Tower, where she and Wat were allowed to join Ralegh. She gave a cry of dismay at seeing him so unlike himself. He had gone quite grey during his imprisonment, and an ague had set into his bones so that he moved with difficulty.

But at the sight of him it was Bess who moved. Like the bird he so often called her, she flew into his arms, thanking God for his life. Wat stood awkwardly by, half frightened by this grim, weary man who looked so different from his gallant father. Then Ralegh smiled and Wat, too, was in his arms, fighting to keep back tears until he saw his parents had both given way to their sorrow.

Together in the small damp room with the mists from the Thames curling up outside the window the three Raleghs clung together, weeping.

But they didn't weep for long. There was too much talking to do. Bess bustled round the bare little room, going to the door to demand that rushes be brought up and a fire kindled. Even so, the room was not pleasant. But to Sir Walter, from the depths of his despair, the sight of his lovely young wife bullying the staff who were supposed to keep the prisoners in order, was like a new lease of life. Unconsciously, he straightened his stooped shoulders and led her into his bedchamber which he would share with Bess, whilst Wat had a little closet off the room allotted to Myers.

'What a miserable little bed,' snorted Bess in disgust. 'Well, for tonight it will suffice.' She looked at Sir Walter consideringly. 'On second thoughts, you're so thin and miserable I'll share your bed. You look as if you could do with me between your sheets to keep you warm.'

Ralegh chuckled with delight at the sweet, teasing note in her voice, but the chuckle turned into a cough. Almost before he knew what was happening he found himself tucked up in bed, with Bess feeding him a delicious savoury stew. Then, as he felt sleep overcoming him, the sofet velvety warmth of his Bess crept into his bed and held him in her loving arms.

For the first time since his arrest, Ralegh slept deeply and dreamlessly, without nightmares.

'Marjory,' Bess told her friend the next day, 'if we can only find some means of support, surely we shall contrive to live without descending into despair?'

Marjory noted with pleasure the martial light in Bess's blue eyes.

'Yes indeed, my dear. Why not apply to Robert Cecil?' Then, as Bess compressed her lips – 'Oh come, Bess, don't be ruled by pride. When Sir Walter was condemned, Cecil wept. Surely he will do all he can to help you now?'

So Bess sank her pride. She visited Cecil

and got his promise of help. She arranged for Sir Alexander Brett, one of the leading doctors of the day, to visit Sir Walter in the Tower. She also got permission for Peter Vanlore, a jeweller and moneylender, to have entry to the Tower on business. There, she gave Sir Walter what remained of her jewellery and this was sold to keep them in relative comfort whilst Cecil did the best he could for them.

'I worry for you here, though, with the plague hot in the Tower,' Sir Walter told her, watching her with contented eyes as she moved round their small living quarters. But Bess was determined to get him comfortably settled – or as comfortably as possible – before setting out to seek further aid for herself and her husband – and, of course, her adored son.

'Cecil has stopped the looting of Sherborne,' Bess was able to proclaim some while later. 'There at least he has stood our friend. And he has told that creature Robert Carr – the King's pretty boyfriend who was given your wine rights or whatever they're called – that he must stop pressing you for debts you are unable to collect from the Tower.'

Ralegh gave an uninterested grunt, bringing a small cry of exasperation from Bess.

'Walter! Whatever are you doing now?'

'Working out a chemical experiment on

paper, except that such a thing is virtually impossible. Later in the year, when the weather improves, the Lieutenant of the Tower has promised me the use of his garden shed for some experiments I would like to make.'

Bess smiled lovingly at the curly grey head. Already her love had come out of his state of shock and exhausted melancholy, and his ever eager brain was searching for something to do. She knew she would have to leave him when the summer months came to go down and make sure all was well at Sherborne.

So when the weather warmed up, and March sunshine danced over the daffodils, Bess and Wat visited Sherborne. How peaceful it was to wander through the grounds once more! How sweet to hear the voices of their loyal and devoted servants, praying that they might soon see their master again!

Here at Sherborne, Bess could pretend that Sir Walter was once more in favour at Court and she and Wat were merely waiting for his return, as they had waited so often. But commonsense soon took over. Her longing to see Sir Walter for herself, to know that he had not slipped back into melancholy, hurried her return to London.

She ran up the steps to Ralegh's apartments in the Bloody Tower in early May, her skin sun-ripened, to find Sir Walter, too, looked more like his old self.

'My darling, you've been getting more air than that from the window – more sun, too,' she exclaimed delightedly, noticing the slight tan on his hands and face.

Ralegh grinned. 'I contrive,' he said airily. 'I now have permission to use the garden as much as I please, and I walk daily on the walls of the Tower so that I can watch the people down below and get proper exercise.'

That same afternoon Bess was privileged to watch her husband's walk. Ralegh set out along the walls, apparently oblivious of the enormous crowd which had gathered to watch him. He walked slowly with bent head, to all appearances absorbed in the book in his hand. But anyone who knew him as Bess did could tell he was acting an enormously enjoyable part – the studious prisoner, taking his chance of an airing, never noticing that he had an audience.

When they climbed into bed that night Bess teased him about his play-acting abilities. He turned to her suddenly, saying hoarsely, 'I have to play-act, my bird. The air of the garden is good, but it's not *my* garden. It's not clean country air. You have the gloss of Sherborne on your skin, and your hair smells of hay and gillyflowers.'

He held her close, his body suddenly hard and demanding against her, and she gave herself to him willingly, glad to know how he had missed her, glad to share with him the waves of passion which took him far from the walls of the Tower and for a short while set them free as birds in the air.

Afterwards, they lay quietly, and Bess talked of the beauties of Sherborne, the messages the servants had sent of hope and love, and the common belief everywhere that King James would soon pardon him.

'Then we will enjoy the beauties of Sherborne together, dear heart,' Bess whispered, tucking her head into his shoulder.

'I have enjoyed the most beautiful thing at Sherborne this night, here in our little cell,' replied Sir Walter, his voice thickened with love and sleep.

Bess smiled softly, joyfully. His mind was sharp as a rapier, her man was really as miraculous as she had boasted. To be able to be free of spirit and thought, when so cruelly constrained, that was a miracle indeed.

'I'm with child,' Bess announced towards the end of August. 'Oh, my love, I've so longed for another babe, be happy with me.'

She thought her news would gladden her husband's heart. After all, here he was alive and fathering another child when less than a year ago he had thought he wouldn't live to see another summer.

However, Ralegh was annoyed and worried. 'The extra expense, my bird, the difficulties of birth in this miserable place!' he exclaimed. 'You'll have to go back to Sherborne, and I hate being separated from you.'

'I'll not go back to Sherborne,' Bess said, affronted. 'As for the extra expense, I'll suckle *this* child myself. Sir Alexander Brett is a great doctor, you've said so many times. He can attend me.'

'Oh well. You're right about Sir Alexander at all events,' muttered Sir Walter. 'As for the rest – we'll see.'

They did see. In February 1605, Bess gave birth, with almost nonchalant ease, to another son. Walter, once the babe and Bess were pronounced in excellent health and spirits, was full of smiles and pleasure. They Christened him Carew, after his Godfather, Richard Carew, who was as much their friend in the Tower as he had been out of it. True to her promise, Bess suckled the child herself.

Their financial affairs were now much more secure. Cecil, who was soon to rise to the rank of Earl of Salisbury, had managed to persuade James to make over the remainder of Sir Walter's estates and possessions in trust for Bess and her boys.

Bess was able to buy a coach so that she could drive out of the Tower with the tiny Carew in her arms and Wat beside her and go to visit friends or buy some of the chemicals essential to her husband's experiments.

The end of the year was given up to the fright James had received from the Gunpowder plot.

Wat, though nearly twelve, was not above playing at being Guy Fawkes until Bess had to speak very sharply to him, especially when an old friend of Ralegh's, Northumberland, was sent to the Tower. Ralegh welcomed him with delight. Northumberland was known as 'The Wizard Earl' because of his keen interest in medicine and astrology, mathematics and, above all, chemistry. To Ralegh it was a heaven-sent chance of improving his own experience in these fields.

Bess, beginning to go about more, found it easier to leave her love in the company of the Earl and later also of Hariot, who was employed by Northumberland.

Bess took Carew to see Marjory and whilst they were cooing over the baby Marjory said suddenly, 'An old friend of ours is in the city, Bess. Remember Frances Hastings, all those years ago when we were mad maids of honour? She got married just before you did.'

Bess gave a cry of delight.

'Invite her here tomorrow afternoon, Marjory, and we'll talk over old times. Is she much changed? But no, don't tell me, I'll see her for myself tomorrow.'

The next afternoon the three women met in Marjory's lodgings. Frances had always been plump. Now she was as round as a ball, but still her eyes twinkled and her tongue was quick to comment.

'Husbands change you and children go on with the unhappy process,' laughed Frances, indicating her girth. In the fifteen years since she and Bess had last met she had given birth to ten children.

'Yes indeed,' agreed Bess. 'I never imagined myself as matronly. I thought forty was the end of the world for a woman, but I shall be forty in less than a year and now it doesn't seem so terrible. If I were dark I might be sadly grey by now.'

'Not if you were me you wouldn't,' laughed Frances. 'I dye my hair with an excellent preparation. Black as a crow's wing, isn't it?'

Marjory and Bess agreed, neither adding that they had gathered at first sight of her that such ebony locks owed something to artifice!

'How are Sir Walter and the children?' Frances asked presently. 'Now I'll settle myself comfortably and you must Tell All!'

Bess laughed at her friend's imperious command but told her story willingly enough.

'Now Sir Walter is as well as he can be, confined as he is,' she ended. 'He has become friendly with the Queen, poor lady. She has an unhappy life, I believe. And, of course, Sir Walter's friendship with Prince

Henry doesn't please King James over-much. But Sir Walter always drew children to him.'

'How do your children go on in the Tower?' asked Frances presently.

Bess's expression changed and became guarded. 'Well enough,' she answered airily. 'Carew is a placid baby and gives Sir Walter a lot of pleasure. He is out of swaddling now of course and into short coats, he'll soon be toddling.'

In the small silence that followed, Marjory handed round refreshments. There were sweet cakes, dishes of candied flower petals and fruit tarts, with a big bowl of straw-berries glazed with sugar for any who liked the fruit.

Bess, helping herself to a strawberry, laughed. 'Alright, I have to admit Wat is a worry to us. He's too full of liveliness for Tower life. He needs the country, plenty of freedom – at least, that's what I think. Sir Walter thinks he is simply over-indulged. However, Wat's a clever lad, fond of his studies as he is fond of games and foolery. Next year he is to enter Corpus Christi as a scholar there. Sir Walter hopes it will do him a great deal of good.'

'The university will calm him down, Bess,' said Marjory comfortingly, and Bess nod-ded.

'He'll be best away from the Tower, it has

overshadowed too much of his life as it is,' she said with quiet feeling.

When she left them, Frances and Marjory stared at each other.

'I told you she's amazing,' Marjory reminded the other woman. 'Even at thirtynine she's as slim and quick-moving as a girl of twenty. I only hope Wat doesn't bring her more trouble. He's ripe for any mischief, Frances.'

'She's had good years,' murmured Frances thoughtfully. 'Now she's having the bad years – and making them seem like a holiday. I pray she continues in this brave spirit, Marjory.'

'I also,' agreed Marjory. 'I wonder if she could have foreseen the future whether she would have married Sir Walter against the Queen's wishes all those years ago?'

'Who can tell?' countered Frances.

But Bess could have told them. She would have suffered far more than she had done for the joys of being married to Sir Walter and for the love she bore her sons.

ELEVEN

LIFE IN THE TOWER

'What a place to give as your home address – The Tower, London,' laughed Wat, helping Bess to pack the books and small personal belongings he would take with him to Corpus Christi.

Bess laughed with him. Wat was almost fourteen, old enough to actually enjoy the thought of leaving home (if you could call the Tower home) and living with a motley assortment of other scholars in the beautiful old university town of Oxford.

'Behave better at Oxford than you have done here this past year or they'll think you yourself had been better confined in the Tower than your poor father,' Bess warned him.

Wat laughed boisterously and then gave Bess a hug that nearly cracked her ribs. He was a fine-looking boy, well grown for his age and with his father's upright, proud carriage. His hair was thick and black and curly, his face had a high glow of colour in the cheeks and his eyes had such thick curling lashes that they gave his face, in repose, an almost womanish beauty.

Unfortunately, thought Bess, his face was rarely in repose. Surely he must be the naughtiest child ever lodged in the Tower? The various Tower officials certainly thought so. Bess had taken him with her on one of her frequent visits to the King. She had knelt before James at Hampton Court to beg a pardon for her husband. Wat, his face far kinglier than the Monarch's, had stood rigidly to attention beside her, despite her attempts to pull him on to his knees.

'Why should I kneel to that drunken sot? That dirty, cowardly, flinching, pawky Scot?' Wat had asked angrily when she had rated him for his behaviour. 'Do you think he would have granted my father liberty if I had done so? You must be mad, mother. He's too taken up with his pretty little boy-friends to bother about the noblest man in the kingdom caged in the Tower. Besides,' he added, abandoning his lofty tone, 'the King's as jealous as all the devils in hell of father, because Prince Henry is forever at the Tower, learning from Sir Walter how to be a soldier and command men.

'Prince Henry notices now how his father smells of spirits. How his skin and linen are always soiled and dirty. James will deny him nothing, but he would deny him access to my father if he had the courage.'

'Queen Anne also visits us here,' said Bess reprovingly. 'The King shows no annoyance that she does so.'

'No, because he doesn't like women, only young men,' replied Wat truthfully, but, Bess thought, with a knowledge beyond his years.

'The King is our one hope for your dear father's release,' she said despairingly, abandoning other arguments. 'He disgusts me as much – probably more – than he disgusts you. But I would do anything – yes, Wat, anything, for your father. He gave up so much for my sake when he married me that if it was in my power to win his release by stooping every day and kissing the King's filthy feet I would do it to further Sir Walter's cause.'

Wat pushed the last book into his trunk and sat back on his heels, seriously regarding his mother's earnest face.

'If I ever marry, I pray it will be to someone as good as you, if such another exists. Really good, I mean, mother. Ready to love, forgive, never accusing my father of leading you into such an existence. Never running away to hide in comfort at Sherborne or with one of my uncles. Mother, I'm not one for pretty speeches, but I love you.'

'I love you, too. Now remember that and be a good student so that I can be proud of you as well. Carew, get your fingers out of that box of comfits! They're for brother Wat, not my little lad.'

Wat pulled the small boy impatiently back from his trunk and smacked him. Carew hit back, then flung himself into Bess's arms, wailing loudly.

Bess sighed. She would miss Wat terribly and so she knew would Sir Walter. But life would certainly be more peaceful without their firebrand son on the premises!

After a while, Bess grew used to seeing only one boy hanging over Sir Walter's arm as he patiently explained the experiment he was doing or the work he was writing. It wasn't Carew, of course – Carew was only two, still more interested in his mother than his father. It was the young Prince Henry who was Sir Walter's staunchest admirer.

Once again, Bess and her coach drove out of the Tower, bound for Sherborne, accompanied by Myers.

As usual there was much to please Bess at Sherborne. She flung herself wholeheartedly into the preparation of housekeeping so that she would be able to take back a store of goods to enliven Sir Walter's diet in the Tower.

Arthur had obtained permission to visit his brother-in-law when he was first imprisoned. So now, knowing that Bess was absent, he would pay his brother-in-law a visit to cheer his solitude.

Arthur enjoyed ill-health in a genteel way at Paulerspury. He no longer attended Court, leaving that to young Nicholas, who had taken the name of his adopted father and was no longer Nicholas Throckmorton but Nicholas Carew.

So whilst Ralegh conducted his experiments, talked to his brother-in-law, wrote leaflets on war and the people's rights, and longed for his wife's return, Bess became mistress of Sherborne once more.

Visitors came to stay and exclaimed that the river looked as though it had always run its present course. The fruit trees, delicately fanned out against the mellowing walls, were laden in their season with peaches, plums and nectarines. The gardens seemed always to be a riot of blossom.

'You should see them gillyflowers Sir Walter brought back from furrin' parts, come the spring,' said one of the gardeners to Bess.

'Why, I made a pot-pourri of their petals, mistress,' cried the housekeeper when Bess sighed over her inability to come down to Sherborne before May. 'You shall take it back to the Tower with you so that Sir Walter may know what sweetness he has brought to England. The gardeners tend his tobacco – does he still enjoy a pipe, my lady?'

'Yes indeed he does,' said Bess, knowing that probably even now he would be sitting at his window waiting for the time of his walk on the walls, and smoking a quiet pipe.

'Ah, this little lad's quiet and good,' sighed the housekeeper, looking fondly down at Carew, still in his baby petticoats. 'But how does our young Master Wat go on at his new school? He'll never be forgotten down here, my lady, for a rare imp he was – and showed no sign of much change, the last time he was here,' she added with a laugh.

'He's still full of tricks,' admitted Bess. 'But he's a very good son. He writes to us regularly and seems to be doing well at his studies. In between the work he tells us he is enjoying an uncommonly fine time.'

'Will he come down here for his summer holidays?' enquired the housekeeper, suddenly remembering that the students 'came down' from Oxford for a summer break.

'He goes first to the Tower, to pay his respects to his father. Then he'll ride down here under the care of his old tutor, Mr Talbot. They'll spend a few weeks here with me, then they'll accompany me back to London before Master Wat returns to his seat of learning.'

When Wat arrived at Sherborne he eyed with pretended horror the pile of things Bess had got ready to take back to her husband.

'Will you go over the things your father asked for, Wat?' said Bess anxiously. 'I can manage all the household things which he will need, but I know very little about the maps and globes, nor the plants he has begged me to bring from the garden.'

Wat, pleased with the responsibility, worked hard to make sure that everything his father would require was packed into the coach. When he had checked and rechecked the great pile of stuff he suggested diffidently to Bess that they might take her coach and go down to Weymouth, just for a few days.

He was afraid the suggestion might make her remember those other trips to Weymouth, with Will Cecil, and Sir Walter suddenly erupting into their quiet days and making everything exciting and adventurous and new. He could remember his mother's face, lighting with laughter like a child's, as they bathed and splashed in the warm waves, and gathered shells and stones and built fortifications of sand and driftwood.

But he underestimated Bess. If she thought of those days it was without regrets. How could she regret such happy memories? It was not to be that Sir Walter could accompany them this year at any rate. Therefore she would take Wat and little Carew, who had never seen the sea.

They didn't spend long at Weymouth, but it was as unchanged and delightful as ever. Wat forgot to despise Carew for a baby and played the games with him that his father had played with Wat and Will Cecil when *they* were young, so long ago.

Bess and her entourage returned to Sherborne for a few days, then the coach was packed, outriders with huge parcels of goods took their places, and Bess and Wat mounted their horses to ride back to London.

This time, Carew sat in front of his brother, playing with the horse's mane and asking endless questions, and Bess could enjoy her last real sight of open countryside until the following summer.

When they got back to their apartments in the Tower, Wat had to leave them to continue his studies. Sir Walter, rejoicing to have once more the company of Bess and their little son, was full of news.

'The country groans under the burden of so unkingly a Monarch,' he whispered joyfully to Bess when they were safe in their bed, away from prying ears.

'Is that to the good?' asked Bess. She had thought it better that the country kept its illusions and didn't compare their present Monarch with 'That great lady whom time hath surprised'. The phrase was Ralegh's, coming spontaneously from his lips during his trial, when he was fighting for his life.

'I believe it's always best to know the truth,' replied Ralegh quietly. 'I have asked that I might be kept in touch with the various expeditions going to Guiana. My requests have been granted and I am fully informed. Nothing has come to light in Guiana as yet, but my hope does not diminish.'

'What you mean is, "Nothing has come to light in Guiana yet because I'm not there myself, telling everyone what to do",' replied Bess, laughing.

Ralegh admitted it, but added drowsily, 'Though here in the Tower there have come to me thoughts that I would never have had, out of captivity. It sometimes seems, Bess, that in prison my mind has been freer than it ever was, when I rode a great horse at the head of a company of men, or sailed the wild oceans searching for adventure and booty, or wooed a beautiful maiden with eyes as blue as April skies and a waist like a willow.'

This was very much what Bess herself had come to believe. She snuggled close to him and said soothingly, 'Good comes, then, from this situation which has been forced upon us?'

'Yes, I believe so,' came his deep, drowsy voice from out of the darkness. 'Who but the man I am today would have a Queen and the Heir Apparent to the throne hanging upon every word he utters? Not the man I was, Bess. He was a man of action, not thought. We must count this a blessing, for when I regain my freedom I shall be a better man.'

Things continued to tread their monotonous round until the year 1609, when a great blow fell on the Raleghs. The lawyers had been looking into the deed of gift leaving Sherborne in trust to Wat. They had found a mistake in the copying of the deed, a mere clerical error, but one which made the deed null and void.

So James stepped in. His favourite, Robert Carr, wanted Sherborne, so Sherborne he should have. Ralegh wrote to Carr pointing out that Sherborne was all he had left to leave his children and that if Carr, in his generosity, would tell the King he didn't covet the place, it could continue in the hands of the family who had made it what it was – the Raleghs.

But Carr did covet it. Bess, always hopeful, knelt once more to the King, raising her beautiful tear-wet eyes to his face and begging that their last remaining possession – and that the most dearly loved – might not be taken from them.

The King shifted uneasily before her. He didn't like women, particularly Ralegh's woman, but his conscience was uneasy. Would he have behaved in this fashion to anyone other than Ralegh? Even to himself he could not say 'I am being fair and kingly'.

'I maun hae it for Carr,' he said in his thick drinker's voice with its broad Scottish accent. But he endeavoured to gild the pill by promising Lady Ralegh £8,000 as purchase money for the life-interest in the estate and a pension of £400 a year during her lifetime and that of her elder son.

Bess left the Court and returned to the Tower. Ralegh wept openly on hearing that Sherborne would be theirs no longer, but agreed reluctantly with Bess that in terms of money King James had been generous.

When Prince Henry heard of the loss of Sherborne his indignation knew no bounds and he vowed to Sir Walter that he would get it back for him, come what may.

'He'll do his best, poor lad,' said Ralegh to Bess. 'But I don't know, my bird. It seems that everything runs against us. I had always dreamed of retiring to Sherborne when I grew too old for an active life. Now even that will be denied me. Sometimes I wonder if I shall ever leave the Tower.'

Bess was dismayed. She had never heard Walter even mention the fear of never leaving the Tower. She found for the first time in her life that she didn't know how to comfort him. It really seemed as if the

King's malignancy would never leave them. Together, they grieved.

When Bess had done all she could to comfort her husband, she made for the person who could comfort her most – Marjory.

'You've no idea how it feels to be quite homeless,' she said disconsolately.

'Don't grieve, Bess,' said Marjory in her soft voice. 'You and Sir Walter love Sherborne, but you mustn't forget Prince Henry. He is worshipped by the people, who can scarcely wait for him to become King in place of his father. If he says he'll restore the place to you, restore it he will.'

'Oh, Marjory, how I hope you're right!' exclaimed Bess. 'You know that Sir Walter is writing a *History of the World*? It is to be for Prince Henry. It would have been published in a year or so, but now the Prince would like more detail added to the earlier part. You can imagine how happy it makes my dearest to oblige. He goes at his book furiously, writing until the candles gutter in their sockets.'

'Yes, I heard Sir Walter was writing a great book,' replied Marjory. 'Tell me, will it be published for everyone to read, or is it for the Prince's eye only?'

'Oh, it will be for everyone to read,' said Bess happily. 'Isn't it funny, Marjory? Now that he is a disgraced prisoner, convicted of treason, everyone wants to read his works.

He is universally admired and the very highest in the realm desire to know him.'

'And Wat? Is he any easier?' enquired Marjory.

Bess stiffened defensively. 'He finds the Tower irksome, but he has friends enough,' she said guardedly.

'And Carew?' enquired Marjory. She felt sometimes that Carew was overshadowed by his brother, so much older and more magnificent than his small self. Carew had Bess's milder colouring, and his temper was more even than Wat's.

'Oh, Carew's fine. Healthy and cheerful. He never worries me, you know, Marjory. I used to worry all the time over Wat. He always seemed to be falling out of lofts or getting into the street on his own, or fighting other little boys. But Carew never falls into scrapes.'

'Perhaps you'd love him more if he did?' said Marjory, greatly daring.

Bess flushed. 'I love him very much. It's just that I have a special love for Wat because he resembles my dear Walter so closely. I can forgive much of his bad behaviour when I remember the tales I've heard of Walter's youth from his cousins and friends.'

But going home towards the Tower, Bess wondered if Marjory was right. Did she secretly despise Carew because he never worried her, never got into mischief? If so, it must be remedied. She entered the Tower that day determined to search for Carew's good points as diligently as she ignored the faults in Wat's character.

TWELVE

THE PROMISE OF FREEDOM

Wat had come down from Oxford at last. He had been involved in a duel (and duelling was forbidden), and the resultant scandal, though hushed up, decided the Raleghs that Wat's education – or at any rate his formal education – had better be called completed.

Wat was delighted. Everything pleased him, his friendship with Prince Henry, even the devotion of his little brother Carew. In that respect the two boys had something beside their mutual love and trust of Sir Walter in common.

Henry also had a little brother. Charles was only six years younger than Henry but nevertheless he idolised his handsome brother, so much cleverer than he.

One day Henry had shyly shown Bess a letter written to him by Charles.

'Sweet, sweet brother,
    I will give you everything I have, both

209

my toys and my books and my cross-bow. Good brother, love me and I shall ever love and serve you.'

When Bess read the note she had to turn away to hide the tears in her eyes. It was so ingenuous – and it reminded her so much of Carew's attitude to Wat. But Wat had no such gentle thoughts for Carew as Prince Henry had for Charles. Wat loved Carew carelessly, accepting his devotion as a matter of course.

Now that Bess had no Sherborne to go to, she took Carew down to Paulerspury or Beddington for the summer months. On the whole she preferred their trips to Beddington. Nicholas was always gay, getting on well with Carew, whereas Arthur lived in a world of enjoyable illness, surrounded by his daughters. Wat accompanied them sometimes, but pronounced the visits dull. For his mother's sake he behaved as well as he could at these times, but was always glad when they were waving their relations goodbye.

When Bess told Wat that Robert Cecil was dying, Wat showed no interest until Bess said she was going to Bath to visit the sick man.

'You'll do no such thing,' blazed out her son, his face suddenly like Walter's used to be when provoked to extreme rage. Bess faced her son coldly.

'I myself have harboured suspicions of Cecil, Wat,' she told him. 'But he is one of my oldest friends. He married another good friend of mine and when she died he never remarried. Whatever his conduct towards us may have been, he has done his best to make amends. I must and shall go to him. Your father could have stopped me, he hasn't tried to do so. Do you dare to interfere where Sir Walter would not?'

Wat didn't answer, but turned sulkily back towards the Tower gardens.

Bess set off for Bath but on the road she learned that Cecil had hired a litter and was being conveyed back to London. She found him at last, alone in a Wiltshire parsonage, except for an elderly servant.

'Robert? It is I, Bess. Poor Robert, you look sadly weak. Can you speak to me?' she whispered, sitting beside his bed.

Cecil didn't answer. From his cold eyes a spark of warmth showed at her gentle tone, and when she lifted one of his cold, limp hands and pressed it between her own soft warm fingers he didn't try to move.

'Listen, Robert,' said Bess urgently in a low tone. 'You had your way to make, your duty to do. Whatever has passed, is past. I cannot say I forgive you for I know of no harm you have done me or mine. If there were any, you have amply made up for it by

211

your efforts since. Now rest, good friend.'

His head turned slowly on the pillow. The pale eyes looked at her enigmatically from his worn face. His breathing was laboured and rasping. But even in his last moments Cecil was not the man to admit a fault and receive a willing forgiveness for it. Instead, he made a feeble sign for her to lower her head.

Thinking he wanted to speak, Bess bent over his wasted form. One thin hand reached up and touched her face gently. That was all.

After this one movement, Cecil sank into a coma from which he never recovered. Bess left the house, telling the servant to take the body to London.

With his death, thought Bess, the last link with the age of the Elizabethans, to which she and Sir Walter belonged, had gone. Ralegh had long since been the last of the noble men who sailed the seas in search of wealth and fame for their country. Drake and Hawkins had died before the old Queen, Frobisher and Howard were long gone. Now it seemed that only she and Sir Walter remained.

A few days after Cecil's death had been made public, Bess was tidying Wat's room when she came across a poem written in her husband's hand. She took it to the window and read it in the light that filtered through the branches of a tree.

'Here lies Hobinol, our pastor while ere,
That once in a quarter our fleeces did
shear,
For oblation to Pan his custom was thus,
He first gave a trifle, then offered up us;
And through his false worship such power
and such gain
As kept him on the mountain and us on
the plain.
Where many a hornpipe he tuned to his
Phyllis,
And sweetly sung Walsingham to's Am-
aryllis.
Till Atropos clapped him, a pox on the
drab,
For (spite of his tarbox), he died of the
scab.'

Bess, wide-eyed with horror, ran to Sir
Walter and speechlessly handed him the
verse.

Ralegh reddened slightly and said apolo-
getically, ''Twas written in a fit of vile
temper, my bird. I thought I'd destroyed it.
I'm sorry you saw it. Look, I'll tear it up and
you can dispose of the pieces.'

He handed the fragments to Bess. As he
put the pieces into her hand he exclaimed,
'My heart's love, don't look so reproachful.
He hated me, you know. One of the servants
said he'd died of the pox and I wrote that

bitter little verse.'

Bess kissed his grey curls. 'I know, it was silly to be so outraged. But I never knew the truth of our suspicions. Perhaps I didn't really want to know. Anyway, let's forget all about it now, shall we?'

But it wasn't possible to forget it. A few days later Bess heard the words being sung in the streets by the Cockneys who had so hated Robert Cecil.

Bess knew better than to blame Sir Walter. She went straight to Wat and accused him of having used the poem without his father's knowledge or consent, to blacken the reputation of a man who was no longer alive to defend himself.

Wat shrugged. 'Think what you will. My actions and thoughts are my own.'

Bess knew upbraiding him would be useless. However, when Ralegh told her that Ben Jonson was taking some young men on the Continental Tour and would oblige them by adding Wat to his party, she agreed with unaccustomed eagerness.

'*Please*, Wat, be as sensible as you can. No fights or brawls. And no disobeying the man who has been good enough to take responsibility for you,' she begged as she saw him off. Wat grinned and kissed her but vouchsafed no reply.

No sooner had Wat returned, at daggers drawn with Ben Jonson for the tricks he had played, than an event of national importance was played out.

James had three children, Prince Henry who was now almost eighteen, Princess Elizabeth, and Charles. A marriage was arranged between Princess Elizabeth and the young Prince of Piedmont. He arrived in November and fell head over heels in love with the enchanting creature. Like Henry, she took after her mother, with richly curling fair hair and a sparkling sense of humour.

She liked her husband Frederick, too, though she could have wished him both taller and older – they were both sixteen. The wedding was a gay affair with dancing and feasting going on day and night, whilst the Prince fell more in love than ever with his young bride, who in future years would be called the Winter Queen of Bohemia. Prince Henry and his sister were great friends, and Elizabeth was pleased when Henry showed unqualified approval of Frederick. But during the marriage festivities it was noticed that Henry didn't seem well. He was persuaded to go to bed, where he grew speedily worse, eventually the fever rising to delirium.

He called constantly for his sister, but she wasn't allowed near him for fear of infection. At Queen Anne's earnest request Ralegh sent his famous cordial that he had concocted during his years of imprisonment in the Tower. But the doctors withheld the life-giving liquid until the last possible moment. After drinking the elixir the fever left the Prince, but he was now too weak to live and after a brief period of consciousness, died.

When Ralegh had despatched the cordial he had done so with his usual note that it was effective against everything but poison. Many believed all their lives that Prince Henry had been poisoned, including his adoring brother Charles.

But the wedding festivities had to go on, though everyone went into mourning. Everyone had loved Prince Henry and looked forward to his reign. Now it would never be.

The Raleghs' grief was deeper by two facts that embittered their thoughts.

Prince Henry had purchased Sherborne from Carr, and made his father promise publicly that he would release Ralegh from the Tower at Christmas, when he came of age.

'Was ever a man so unlucky,' mourned Bess. 'To have his Prince, his promise of home and liberty snatched from his grasp once more.'

For, to James, death cancelled all promises. He gave Sherborne back to Carr and made no mention of Ralegh's possible release. When Christmas came, Walter, Bess and Carew, now breeched and a proper little boy, tried to forget their troubles and made as merry as possible in the Tower. But to Bess and Walter, the wine of Sherborne and freedom had once more been dashed from their lips before they could taste it.

Bess couldn't keep her sorrow hidden. She clung close to Sir Walter in bed and whispered, 'Oh, my dear love, but for the death of poor Henry we should this night have slept beneath our own roof. Safe at Sherborne with those that love us.'

'Ah well, who knows?' murmured Ralegh. 'The King of Denmark is now asking for my release to him, to become his chief admiral. James may be glad to get rid of me at any price. I wouldn't mind starting a new life in a new country.'

Bess could only marvel once more at his resilience. Ralegh was nearly sixty, yet he could look to life in another country as an exciting adventure. For herself, she would go – and willingly – where he led.

'But what will happen to the *History of the World* now?' she wondered as she fell asleep. She needn't have worried. For Prince Henry's sake, Ralegh would finish the book. It was written for the dead prince and would serve as a princely epitaph.

So whilst her husband finished his book, and Wat went off with a friend, Bess took

Carew down to Paulerspury.

She and Anna were sitting, one sunny afternoon, in the sunny gardens, discussing the latest London scandal – the divorce of Frances Howard and her remarriage to Carr.

'How James must miss Robert Carr,' remarked Anna presently. She was careful not to remind Bess that the hated couple lived at the Raleghs' beloved Sherborne.

'Anna, you know *nothing*,' gasped Bess, laughing. 'He's got a new favourite now, rather a charming young man. His name is George Villiers, but James calls him "Steenie", short for Stephen, because James says he's just like St Stephen! He's a friend to us, and always petitioning the King for us.' She laughed again. 'Sometimes I feel almost sorry for James. Everyone he loves seems to like Sir Walter, and King James has a hatred for us Raleghs which nothing will ever appease.'

'I wonder where Catherine has taken Carew?' mentioned Anna, anxious to take Bess's mind off the King. 'She is so fond of children and would have loved a brother.'

The two women, so different yet such good companions, got up and walked through the estate into a delightful little copse where they found Catherine and her cousin.

Their summer interlude over, Bess nursed

her husband through a bad winter in the Tower. He had breathed in chemical fumes which affected his health, and he aged during the long winter in the confines of the Tower.

Then, in the summer of 1615, Wat once more caused them anxiety. They heard from Arthur that his friend, Sir Henry Wotton, had met Wat and a friend at Utrecht. They had gone there to fight a duel – they had already fought once in England. But this fight proved more serious for Wat, who was refused permission to return to England.

'Oh my poor lamb, that hot temper is always getting him into trouble,' sighed Bess, and Walter said resignedly, 'I suppose I'd better write to Prince Maurice. Perhaps he will give Wat a place in his service, for my sake.'

So, for the time being, Wat was out of England and unable to return.

Then the hints and rumours that the Raleghs had hardly dared to believe came true. King James, desperately short of money, released Ralegh from the Tower to undertake the voyage to Guiana, in the hope that he would bring back gold.

Bess hired a house in Broad Street and was there to greet him, flinging herself into his arms and weeping at the wondering pleasure in his eyes as he gazed about him.

'Where – where is your pardon, my love?

Let me see it,' begged Bess at last.

Sir Walter smiled wryly. 'So would I like to see it,' he told her. 'There is no pardon for me, Bess, until I return from the Guiana voyage, decks heaped with gold.'

'But – but who will take ship with a man still branded of treason?' asked Bess. 'And on such a dangerous mission. Oh, my darling, don't go! Stay here in London or we'll go to a quiet house in the country. Guiana will be danger enough with the Spaniards so thick thereabouts – if your men aren't loyal, you will be lost.'

'My bird, I *must* go to Guiana,' Sir Walter told her. 'Why, Keymis is almost certain he has found the goldmine. I have to go. Once my first seasickness has passed, there's nothing in the world more free than the decks of a tall ship, with the stars above and the water below, and no king other than the King of Heaven to interfere with your courses.'

Bess held him tightly, compressing her lips and holding back traitorous tears.

'Freedom means so much more to a man than a woman, I suppose,' she said at last in a voice that only trembled slightly. 'Well, Carew and I will enjoy living in this fine house, and will pray daily for your safe and speedy return.'

'Mine and others,' said Sir Walter triumphantly. 'Wat is pardoned to return to the country and take the position of captain on one of the other ships of the fleet. When he returns from the Continent what a bustle there will be, preparing the ships for the voyage.' He laughed. 'We haven't got the ships yet, so don't be sad, Bess, I'll be with you for a while yet. And Wat also, my bird.'

But Bess was gazing at him with widening eyes. 'Wat? But he's no sailor. No soldier, either. Sweetheart, he's so impetuous, so thoughtless. Don't imperil the enterprise by taking our son, I beg you.'

'He'd never forgive either of us if he didn't go,' Sir Walter said gently. 'Don't fear, Bess, I'll take good care of your first-born.'

Bess bit back the obvious retort that Damerei had been her first-born, and he was dead. She imagined Wat's fury if he were denied the chance of seeing the foreign lands he had always dreamed about.

With a sigh, she thought she had never been able to deny him anything. She would be powerless to deny him this chance of a marvellous adventure.

'Perhaps it will cool his hot blood,' she said, patting her husband's strong hand. Then the words returned to her with another meaning, and fear gripped her throat. She stared before her, seeing all she loved wrecked on an alien shore, and she unable to raise a finger to help.

'What's the matter, my bird?' asked Sir

Walter. 'Seeing ghosts?'

With a tremendous effort Bess forced her fears to the back of her mind and said lightly, 'I'm just wondering whether a sword or a cutlass would best please Wat.'

'A present for his first voyage? Well thought of, Bess. And either would please him,' answered Ralegh. 'Our Wat has ever loved a fight.'

THIRTEEN

TASTE OF FREEDOM

Bess was happy with Sir Walter's happiness in his freedom. For herself, she thought she had never worked – or begged – so hard. Money was needed for the ships, the crews, the supplies. In between attacking the work, Sir Walter wandered round London, the city so changed in his thirteen years of incarceration.

'The people worry me,' he admitted to Bess after his first walk through the streets. 'They seem to press all about. And there is so much noise, so many carriages, horsemen, beggars, idlers. So much more of everything. It seems that riches and poverty have both increased a hundredfold, and poor old London is bursting at the seams.'

'You have to walk as far as Islington to hear a cuckoo now,' quoted Bess, smiling slightly.

'But, my bird, it's all so unnecessary. If only these poor people could be persuaded to go to my colonies, how much happier would be their lot,' sighed Sir Walter. 'If the King thought for his people, he wouldn't just allow such misery to exist outside his very palace walls.'

'Why, James rarely appears in public. You know he fears crowds and people pressing round him. They say even the Court is less open than it was in Elizabeth's day,' reminded Bess.

'Well, of course I can't say much about the Court since I am forbidden access there.'

'You know Ben Jonson. Would you like to ask him to dine here?' suggested Bess. Ralegh nodded eagerly, then changed his mind.

'I don't really know how dangerous I am to people yet, unpardoned as I am,' he explained. 'But I'll go to Jonson's house and ask him to dine with me at the Mermaid Tavern, as we did in the old days.' He shook his head sadly. 'Only Ben and me left of that glad company,' he mourned. 'Do you remember the others, Bess? Spencer, with his head full of dreams. Harriot, with his head full of science and questions, Marlowe, with his head full of...'

'Seditious thoughts and too much wine,' interrupted Bess crisply. 'I know you'll laugh at me, love, but Marlowe died the year I gave birth to Wat. They are alike in their badnesses, and I've often wondered if my fear of Marlowe's influence on you affected Wat whilst he was in the womb.'

'Superstitious woman!' laughed Ralegh, giving her a slight hug.

But Bess had sowed strange thoughts in Ralegh's mind. Wat did have that wildness that Marlowe had once possessed. The air of having more life than other people, so that it spilled out in wild and reckless action. But Marlowe had never really had a chance. The son of a shoemaker, he was quick to take offence where none was intended. Also he drank, whereas Wat was as abstermious as his father.

But when Ralegh joined Ben Jonson at the Mermaid some weeks later, his thoughts were troubled by the seeds of doubt Bess had planted in his mind.

Ben Jonson didn't help much.

'You're taking that son of yours on your voyage? Truly, those years in the Tower *must* have turned your brain,' he declared. 'I took him to the Continent for you – remember? Walter, the tricks he played, the way he behaved! I'm a broadminded man, but a youth who ties a lady's favour to his codpiece and wears it at a noble assembly – Walter, that youth is no person to entrust with your men and their lives, let alone your own life.'

'Did he do that?' said Sir Walter, his brow darkening. 'He needs the voyage to Guiana to teach him what suffering can be.'

'Yes, he did that and worse. He got me drunk – blind drunk – dead drunk – and stretched me out on a wheelbarrow. Then he wheeled me round the streets of Paris, telling those devout Catholics I was a livelier image of the Crucifixion than any they had.'

'He must bear a charmed life – it was enough to get him hung,' muttered Ralegh, shocked by the sacrilege as much as by his friend's embarrassment.

'If I hadn't been responsible for him, I'd have led the hanging party by the end of that Tour,' sighed Jonson. 'I tell you, Walter, he may be your son – well, it's in his face plain for all to see – but the devil has some part in him. I would counsel you against the voyage, old friend, only I know it would go against your very nature to draw back. But I must counsel you against taking your son.'

'My wife – did you tell Lady Ralegh how Wat behaved on the Continent?' asked Ralegh after a pause.

Jonson shook his head sadly. 'She's a fond mother. She coloured to the roots of her hair and tried to say he was full of spirit, but the words stuck in her throat and she looked so bewildered and hurt that I kept the worst from her.'

'Poor Bess, what a child she's given birth to,' said Ralegh quietly. 'Yet she takes little comfort from Carew, who is good and quiet and obedient. I tell you, Jonson, I feel safer having Wat by me than leaving him with his mother. Carew is only eleven, but I swear I leave Bess in his charge more happily than I would leave her in Wat's care.'

'How does your victualling and manning go?' asked Jonson presently.

Ralegh sighed. 'The captains, most of them, are good men. They have to be, to sail with a man under the threat of death for treason. But the sailors are the scum of all the ports in the West Country. The journey is long and hard and they have no faith in this old eagle,' touching his breast lightly, 'preferring to place their faith in younger men.'

'What younger man would take on such a mad voyage as this?' asked Jonson mockingly. 'Perhaps some of Wat's wildness is inherited after all.'

'I *must* do it, Ben,' Ralegh said earnestly. 'You understand that, don't you?' And his old friend had to admit, reluctantly, that he understood.

When Wat returned to his parents he seemed so full of enthusiasm for the Guiana voyage that he had no time for trouble.

He and Sir Walter went round the ports persuading men to join their fleet. He helped Bess in her never-ending search for some new source of revenue, borrowing, selling their plate, using their income from the sale of Sherborne all in one fell swoop, thinking never of saving for 'after the voyage'.

Bess, to be sure, did think of it. But it would have been cruel to say anything of that nature to her husband. He was so sure, so certain, that he would come back, decks laden with gold and the holds heavy with treasure.

One evening before the start of the voyage, Sir Walter took Wat with him to a solemn dinner party, where the talk would be of the possibilities of the voyage and the way the money had been spent.

'You will behave, Wat?' begged Bess. 'Oh, you look fine in cream-coloured velvet, my lamb. Now, you'll behave well, for my sake as well as your father's?'

'I'll do my best, mother,' replied Wat.

The dinner was long and every bit as dull as Bess had feared it would be. Wat, like his father, only drank sparingly and ate fastidiously so the meal itself held little interest for him. He was the youngest person present by many years and kept quiet for hours, or so it seemed to him.

At last a lull came in the conversation. Wat forgot his promises to his mother, his longings to be like his dignified father.

'I was with a lady this morning,' he began easily enough, 'who seemed quite willing to be more than friends with me. I kissed and caressed her and was about to enjoy her

228

when she thrust me back, saying, "Nay, I cannot, for your father was here before you".'

There was a shocked silence. None was more shocked than Ralegh himself. Then he turned and hit Wat across the face. Wat stared at him silently for a moment and Ralegh wondered in a nightmare what he should do if the boy struck him back. But Wat merely turned and hit the face of the man sitting next to him, saying nonchalently, 'Box about. 'Twill come to my father anon.'

Ralegh apologised stiffly for his son's ill behaviour and left. Back in the house he ordered Wat to his room in tones of sternest displeasure and when they were in their own chamber repeated the tale of the evening to Bess.

Poor Bess, torn between laughter and horror at her son's wickedness, could only stare at Sir Walter in dismay.

'Tell him you won't have such an unruly mischief maker with you on the voyage to Guiana,' she was beginning, when there was a knock on the door.

Sir Walter opened it and Wat stepped in and dropped on one knee before his father.

'Please forgive me. I don't know what got into me – I never mean to say such things, father. Certainly I never meant to bring you to ridicule for having such a son. Sometimes it seems as though another voice speaks from my mouth. Forgive me.'

Walter said quietly, 'You are young. Heedless, perhaps. But not, I'm sure, deliberately wicked. I forgive you. Leave us now, my son.'

Wat left the room with his swift, arrogant stride and Ralegh gazed at Bess, a slight smile hovering at the corners of his mouth.

'Our eldest son, my bird, really makes me feel old, but I'm sure this adventure will be the making of him. To know me completely my own master and the leader of men may lead him to have more respect for me.'

'Oh, my love, he must respect you – all who know you do so,' laughed Bess. 'But I must admit he makes me feel old, too. Every grey hair on my head turned white this evening. How the young punish you when they come to years of discretion – or should I say indiscretion?'

'You should,' said Ralegh emphatically as they got into bed. He snuffed the candle and they lay side by side, each knowing the other's anxious thoughts but unable to give the necessary comfort.

Shortly after the disastrous dinner party the Raleghs made their way to London Pool, where the ships for the expedition had been built. Ralegh and Wat sailed them down to the coast whilst Bess and Carew rode down to the West Country to see them off on their momentous voyage.

To Ralegh's pleasure, once out of the metropolis, Wat behaved as he had done when they first started work. He rounded up and drilled his men with all the energy of a sheepdog dealing with a recalcitrant flock, and Ralegh admitted to Bess that he seemed able to cope with all the difficulties that had occurred so far on land.

They had left Wat dealing with the ships, Myers in charge of Carew, and had ridden up the coast to see some of the little bays where Walter himself had played as a child. Now they stood on the shore of one of the little beaches, leaving the horses cropping the short sweet grass on the cliff.

Bess knelt down beside a pool, heedless of her wide skirts dipping into the water, and poked a curious finger at a hungry scarlet anemone endlessly beckoning with its tentacles. Ralegh showed her how to tease it with a tiny empty shell, which was seized and then spat out again in disgust.

'You'll see stranger sights than this by far, once you're off and away,' sighed Bess, suddenly filled with envy.

Ralegh looked across the pool at her, seeing the reflected ripples on the white skin beneath her chin, the look of childish pleasure mixed with envy at the thought of the great discoveries he might make whilst all the time her calm blue gaze was on him, a little enquiring.

'You are beautiful, my bird,' Ralegh said tenderly. 'You carry your age as well as you carry your figure. When I think of the worries and fears that have been your lot ever since you married me, it's a wonder to me that you still want to be with me all the time, far less envy me my voyage into the unknown. Most wives would rail at being left once again, at having their eldest son torn from their sides when he was scarce out of leading strings, but not you. You have a generous spirit, my bird.'

Bess, blushing and laughing, said lightly, 'What stuff! If you could read some of my thoughts about King James now—' she didn't finish the sentence for there was no need. Laughing, they began the return walk across the beach, Ralegh leaning on his stick. Bess felt for a moment the freedom Sir Walter must be feeling, as the wind touched her cheek, lifting a strand of her hair and ruffling the long fur-trimmed cloak she wore.

All the way back to Plymouth they were silent, each comfortably aware of the other's presence, but deep in their own thoughts.

'What if he comes back without the gold?' drummed through Bess's mind, when it was not confused by the worse thought, 'What if he never comes back?'

Ralegh's mind dwelt on the beauties of

England and of the offer he had received to run his fleet into a French port, if he should hear bad tidings on his return voyage. He seriously considered it, as a man must. He knew that should he return without gold he would at the least be imprisoned once more. In France he would be a free man. No, more than merely free. A revered man, to whom all would turn for advice and help. It would be balm to his spirit, wounded so often by neglect. Bess could come to him there, with Carew.

Ralegh didn't often consider the possibility of not returning laden with gold, but he had been talking to Sir Francis Bacon, that astute man of affairs. Although Sir Francis had assured him that he was as good as pardoned, he had stressed both the King's need for money – he was £700,000 in debt – and his hopes of a Spanish marriage for his heir to the throne, Prince Charles.

'The Spanish wench would bring a noble dowry with her,' Sir Francis hinted. 'So the King is not unwilling to consider the alliance. And he is *most* unwilling that Spain should be annoyed in any way by your voyage.'

'I've already signed a paper guaranteeing on pain of death that I will not take Spanish life or property,' protested Ralegh. 'But if for some reason we cannot get at the gold – if the Spaniards are between us and the mine – then I shall try for the Plate fleet. Imagine, two and a half millions from Mexico brought to the King's feet.'

'You'd be a pirate,' warned Sir Francis Bacon, half laughing.

'What! Who ever heard of a pirate for millions?' protested Ralegh.

Now, as he rode along the winding country lanes beside his Bess, he thought of other talks. It was an open secret that the King had told the Spanish Ambassador, Gondemar, of the intentions of the expedition, though it had been given out that Ralegh sailed for Virginia.

What else had the King told? wondered Ralegh uneasily. The King fawned on Gondemar like a lick spittle spaniel. Ralegh remembered the weak, frightened eyes, the malice in the King's gaze when directed at himself. If he's told all – he thought in sudden alarm, then dismissed the fear. How could anyone, even King James, betray a man and his followers to what would be ambush and probably a horrible death?

So despite himself Ralegh pondered on life in France for himself and his family. And despite the mad March breeze, the sunshine and the feel of the horse moving under her, Bess remembered tales of Spaniards she had heard as a child, tales Ralegh had told her himself of the furies of Orinoco and the wild jungle which had to be fought for every foot one gained.

Unlike her husband, she had little belief that Keymis had actually discovered the whereabouts of a gold mine. But she had infinite, implicit faith in Ralegh. If there was gold to be found, he would find it. She knew the commonly expressed fears amongst the crews that the King was too fond of a Spaniard and might reveal too much. They didn't know he had forced Ralegh to give him lists of the numbers of his men, amounts of provisions taken on board each vessel, where they would stop for fresh water and revictualling, and where they would land in Guiana.

If they had known so much, who would have trusted James enough to sail under Ralegh? So Ralegh mentioned this last fact to no one. He for one would have to put complete trust in James and hope that for the sake of the gold he coveted James would not betray him to Spain.

Shortly after their ride together, rumours began to fly that the King would take fright and the voyage would be stopped. So the Raleghs finalised the victualling of the last ship. Bess had to enter into a bond to pay for the groceries for Wat's ship, Ralegh had to sell the last of the family plate. But at last all was ready.

Bess stood on the quayside gripping

young Carew's hand hard in her own and waving her handkerchief towards the ships as they gallantly sailed into the Atlantic.

'See, Carew? Isn't it a brave sight?' she said as cheerfully as she could. She had no need to lift him up to catch a last glimpse of his father, for already Carew, though only twelve, was as tall as his mother.

The little fleet sailed out over the choppy green waves, their sails bellying fitfully in the rough wind, the colour of them changing from snow white to blue as shadows of clouds raced across the water. Bess could see the bustle on decks scrubbed white in preparation for the voyage. She fancied she could pick out Wat's figure on his vessel, but on board the *Destiny* there was no sign of Ralegh.

'My poor darling,' Bess murmured. 'His first time at sea for more than a dozen years and it has to be rough. I hope he isn't too seasick.'

Carew, standing beside her, didn't hear her words. His eyes strained after the fleet. His heart and soul went out to it. If only, oh if only he was a few years older and could share with his father and brother this moment of triumph! For a moment he almost believed his longing would draw him after the ships like a magnet draws iron, then he shook himself and came back to the world of reality.

Now his mother was turning away from the quayside. They were walking slowly, still hand in hand, across the green of the Hoe. Carew became aware that hot tears of disappointment were welling up in his eyes. He sniffed surreptitiously and peeped up at his mother to see if she had noticed his moment of unmanly weakness.

Bess was looking straight ahead. The wind had caught her hair, but she let it stream behind her unheeded. Carew thought she looked like some magnificent figurehead, braced against the wind, her profile calm and serene, her lips firmly closed.

Then he looked again. Tears were running from her eyes and being whipped across her cheeks, though her expression was unchanging.

Was it the wind, wondered Carew, or was his mother crying without knowing it? She gave none of the usual signs of weeping. Her cheeks were unflushed, her mouth didn't pull itself into ugly shapes, as Carew knew his own did when he wept. He watched and wondered, as the steady flow of tears continued down the serene face.

She doesn't look like a figurehead but like the statue of a saint, thought Carew suddenly. A statue that had learned to shed tears.

But then they reached the top of the Hoe and for a moment they turned and looked back.

Below them on the sea of green, topped with white crests, the fleet already looked miles away. Small, bright and brave but so insignificant compared with the mighty emptiness of that vast stretch of water.

Bess looked down at Carew at last, but he doubted if she really saw him.

'The dice is cast,' she murmured. 'Now we must wait, wait, wait until we know whether we have won or lost.'

'I wish I were with them, mother,' said Carew tentatively. 'Would not you like to be a man and go a-venturing into the unknown lands? See the parrots swinging from the trees, and the natives, and the creatures? I'd like to taste the strange fruits, and help to find the gold, and pick riches from the very rocks, as father used to say.'

'Ah, women were made for waiting – you only have to wait until you're a man, Carew. We women wait for ever. Come, the wind is cold.'

Clasping his hand more gently, she set off in the direction of their lodgings, to take horse for Broad Street where they would – wait.

FOURTEEN

THE WAITING GAME

'Have you heard anything from Sir Walter, Bess?' asked Arthur, filling his pipe with tobacco and leaning back in his chair.

Bess had yielded to his entreaties and gone down to Paulerspury for the end of the summer months.

'Yes, I had a letter from Ireland. Do you remember Lismore, in Cork?'

'Oh, too well,' Arthur chuckled. 'Walter never stopped talking about the way the potatoes flourished over there and how the azane lillies and gillyflowers bloomed. Boyle has the place now, hasn't he? It is there Walter writes from?'

'Yes,' said Bess, smiling over their shared memories. 'I never saw it, you know, but I heard of his estates and how the Irish sneered at the potatoes. Yet already Walter says the common people are growing them for food. But the Earl of Cork regales Walter on all of the best.'

'But what's he doing in Ireland, my dear sister? Don't tell me the fellow has seen sense at last and decided to call the whole mad scheme off?' enquired Arthur, without much hope.

'Oh Arthur, of course not,' said Bess reproachfully. 'He and the rest of his fleet have been badly knocked about in the gales – what a dreadful summer it's been to be sure – and they are mending the ships and revictualling. Walter says the Earl's generosity is wonderful. He has given them oxen, beer, even money. And just for the officers a thirty-two gallon cask of his own whiskey.'

'But Walter rarely drinks, neither does Wat,' objected Arthur, thinking how he would have relished a share in that part of the Irish bounty.

'He may need to, when the weather is very rough and cold spirits can warm a man,' said Bess, laughing.

Arthur snorted and moved over to the leaded window. Although it was only early September the fire in the room had misted over the glass against the cold from outside. Arthur rubbed a peephole for himself in one of the small panes and peered out.

'Brrr, raining again,' he announced. 'Bess, I declare I almost envy Walter and Wat the weather they will shortly be enjoying.'

'Walter could do with some tropical

sunshine after the long years spent in the damp of the Tower,' agreed Bess doubtfully. 'But he isn't as young as he was to stand up first against the incessant drenchings and chills of the storms and then against the blazing heat and fevers of the tropics.'

She got up from her chair and moved restlessly to the window, peering out as Arthur had done.

'Oh, God's wounds! If it doesn't stop raining soon I shall die of a melancholy,' she announced in a vicious tone which sounded very much alive.

Some weeks later Bess was to be one of many to hear further news of her husband. A Captain Bayley of Ralegh's fleet had deserted with his ship and was back in England, spreading reports that Ralegh had taken to piracy.

Bess, remembering some of the things that Walter had said about one or two of the men, was furious at the complacency with which the news was received, one of the Privy Councillors going so far as to publicly apologise for Ralegh's actions, assuring everyone that King James would redress any losses and punish Ralegh for his sins.

Fortunately, friends of Ralegh's rallied round and tried to veryify Bayley's reports. His own crew stood up in public and said that the only acts of piracy were when Bayley himself had tried to seize four

French ships and Ralegh had not allowed him to do so. Bayley, furious at being baulked of his prey, had taken himself and his ship's company back to England in a huff, there to do as much damage to Sir Walter as he could.

Bess had another letter, telling her that Ralegh was very weak with fever – or rather had been, for he was now strong enough to pen her a long letter.

The biggest piece of good news he had for her was that Wat was not only well and in the best of spirits, but he didn't suffer from seasickness like his father, and the heat actually seemed to agree with him.

'That doesn't surprise me,' said Anna darkly in the privacy of their bed. 'A devil like Wat should feel at home in a furnace like that Guiana.'

'Anna, Anna, don't talk unkindly of the boy,' murmured Arthur. 'He is the pride and joy of my sister's heart. Besides, Walter seems to think the voyage will be the making of him. Think of our children, Anna, always free to run and play and shout. Poor Wat was in the Tower or in the homes of others, with only his pride to save him. How should you expect him to be other than difficult?'

'Carew was *born* in the Tower, and he's a good lad. When young Wat can stay here for a week and not get up to some devilry I'll believe him reformed,' stated Anna firmly.

When he would have remonstrated with her again, she rolled over and presented him with her substantial back. It was no good continuing the argument, so Arthur pulled the sheets up round his ears and muttering that he hoped she had remembered the two absent Raleghs in her prayers, went to sleep.

Christmas came, and Carew received the little horse he had wanted – a gelding of Arthur's own breeding, very high spirited and full of mettle.

Bess watched him with his first horse – previously he had ridden ponies – and pride stirred in her heart. Maybe he was more her son than Walter's, to look at, but he was full of his father's proud and determined spirit without having to continually assert himself, as did his elder brother.

Bess thought her nicest Christmas present was another letter.

'They're in Guiana! They've arrived!' she called in a high voice. 'Carew, Arthur, Anna, they're alive and well, though Walter still has the fever on him and...'

But suddenly the gaily decorated room and the tall candles began to tilt and blur. Bess clutched wildly at space, then sank into darkness.

She came round sprawled on the rushes, with Arthur burning horseshoe shavings under her nose and Carew's worried face close to her own.

'Oh my goodness, I fainted!' she exclaimed. 'Do you know, I always used to envy people who could faint, but I don't any more, it's a most unpleasant sensation.'

She sank into a chair and rested her head in her hands. 'What made me do that?' she wondered. 'Why should I ... Oh God, the letter, I was reading the letter. Where did I drop it? What did I do with it?'

'Don't be in a worry, mother, I have it safe,' said Carew quickly. He ran his eyes down the pages. 'Here is the gist of it, for you'll not read it tonight. Father's writing is still a bit wobbly because he's not yet conquered the weakness that followed the fever. However, they've met with friendly natives and the one that lived with father in the Tower – do you remember, mother? Harry he called himself in England – well, he's taking care of father and making him well again after the voyage.

'Father says he is keeping a journal so we can read for ourselves how they spend each day, and that he is not going to take part in the expedition to the mine because he would only impede their progress, being still weak from fever. Instead, he will guard the river mouth in case the Spaniards try to cut them off from their ships. That's about all, mother dear. The rest is all about the birds and animals and plants he is finding. You can read it for yourself tomorrow. Now, mother, Aunt Anna is going to help you upstairs, and then Myers will take care of you. I'll guard the letter, you need not fear, and you shall have it as soon as you've breakfasted.'

Bess was about to protest, to take the letter from him, when she realised this was an important moment for Carew. He was taking care of her, making sure she didn't over-excite herself.

'Thank you, my love,' she said meekly, giving him a smile of gratitude and affection. She let Anna lead her from the room, whilst Arthur called for the faithful Myers to attend her.

Carew, proudly taking the letter to his room and placing it carefully beneath his clothes on the joint stool, got into bed feeling that perhaps being left at home wasn't too bad. It could, after all, have been worse if Bess had been by herself, left to face the worrying months ahead with no son to protect her.

As he lay in the darkness, Carew thought how much better it would have been if they could have been at Sherborne. By the most irritating twist of fate, Sherborne had been offered by the King to George Villiers, his present favourite and a young man who had already proved himself a good friend to the Ralegh family.

Thinking that if he refused the house it

would revert to its rightful owners, young Villiers, created Duke of Buckingham by his infatuated monarch, refused Sherborne. The manor was given instead to Digby, Earl of Bristol, and now it was Carew Ralegh who was tempted, and frustrated, by Sherborne, as his father had been and always would be. It seemed as though Sherborne would tantalise the Ralegh family for ever, like a beautiful, much-loved woman who now seems ready to give herself, then coyly withdraws.

'But perhaps, if father returns with great riches, Sherborne will belong to us Raleghs once again,' murmured Carew sleepily to himself. 'I shall do my best to regain possession of the estate when I'm a man, if it's not already in father's hands. He made it out of a half-ruined castle, it *should* belong to a Ralegh.'

Lying in bed, he suddenly remembered the letter. He rolled out from between the sheets and thrust a taper into the dying embers. Then he lit a candle and began to read. Oh the romance of it, he sighed to himself. The beauty, the cruelty, the danger, that father and Wat were living through.

Sitting on the bed scanning the pages, his light brown hair curling across his broad forehead, he looked for a moment rather like his father. The same resolution, the dancing light of excitement, shone from his dark blue eyes as had gleamed so often in Ralegh's bright black ones.

Then a draught blowing the candle flame and a nightbird calling brought Carew back to the present. Reluctantly he realised he was tired and getting cold. The visions of the steaming green jungle, beautiful native girls and solemn wise old chiefs faded from his brain. Instead he saw the rush-strewn floor, the curtains round his bed that he had pulled back with an impatient hand, and his adolescent legs turning goose-fleshed with the cold.

He bundled himself back into his still warm bed and thrust the letter under his pillow. His last waking thought was a child's thought once more.

'I hope they bring me back a parrot.'

They did not bring back a parrot. Neither did they come at once themselves. First of all, Bess had to receive another letter from Sir Walter. In the spring of 1618, feeling herself too far from the heart of things at Paulerspury, Bess and Carew returned to the house in Broad Street. It was there that the letter was delivered.

Bess looked at the handwriting and said thankfully to Carew, 'The writing is a little steadier. Pray God your father is stronger.'

She began to read and Carew, watching, saw her whiten to the lips. Her eyes, wide open in staring horror, seemed fixed. Carew knew something was wrong and he moved to catch her if she fell. But she didn't move. She stood as if frozen, her lips not moving, her eyelids not blinking.

Carew cried, 'Mother, mother, what's wrong?' but she didn't answer, nor did her gaze move from the words on the paper before her.

Myers, running into the room at Carew's urgent call, helped him to lift Bess gently on to a chair.

'Come, my dearest, come, my lady,' said Myers, chaffing the cold hands which lay so still in her mistress's lap. 'Come, my little one, what's the matter with you? Is it illness? Shall I fetch the doctor to see to you?'

'It's the letter. She's dropped it under the chair,' said Carew briefly. 'It's from father. Shall I read it, Myers?'

Myers nodded quickly, whilst ordering a servant to bring a hot posset for my lady, for she was ill.

Carew picked up the letter and read. Myers, taking more notice of her beloved mistress than the boy, heard him give a hoarse gasp and sit down abruptly on a velvet covered stool.

'Myers,' he said in a hushed whisper, 'Wat is killed. Father is alright, but Wat is killed.'

Myers turned round quickly, dismay on her round, rosy face.

'Before God, is my mistress never to have

ought but sadness in her life?' she cried. 'Why, Carew, Master Carew, she's in a state of shock. Send Robert the footman for Sir Alexander Brett.'

But Bess moved her head slightly on the cushions and her pale lips formed the word 'No'.

She held out one hand and caught hold of Carew, holding him tightly. A servant brought the tall silver gilt cup of steaming posset and Carew held it to his mother's lips. As she sipped he could see the faint colour returning to her cheeks.

When she had finished the drink she turned to Myers, saying in a dulled voice, 'My good Myers, Master Wat is killed in a battle somewhere on that dreadful continent. I can read no more for a while. But I'm alright now, no need to send for the doctor. Carew, I must get away from the house for a little. Will you walk with me?'

Myers demurred, even cried a little, but Bess was gentle but adamant. She must go outside. So she was wrapped in her warmest cloak and together Bess and Carew walked down to the river because it was near water, she explained, that she felt closest to Sir Walter.

Bess tried to pull herself together and talk sensibly to Carew about the way his brother had died. It was a noble death, she said, leading a hopeless charge against the

249

Spaniards.

When they had gone a little way she got the letter out and read it aloud. Carew gave a little cry of distress on hearing that the faithful Keymis had committed suicide after the return of his unsuccessful attempt to find the mine, and the death of young Wat Ralegh.

'Now father will come home without the gold,' said Carew slowly. He looked up at the pale blue sky dappled with clouds. The trees overhead, leafless still, were full of promise. They seemed in some strange way to add to his hurt. The beautiful April day was not less beautiful because Wat was dead. The weather should be dull and overcast, he thought passionately, because his handsome, gay brother was dead and his father would be returning home tired, sad and dispirited. And yet with its heartless gaiety the breeze snatched at his hat and teased his mother's fringed cloak.

'Look, Carew, how the swans sail over the water,' said Bess, pointing to a group of the birds gliding across the river like a miniature flotilla. 'They say when swans die they sing. I'm sure Wat died like a swan – fierce, proud, but with his heart singing.'

'Wat died encouraging his men to fight for San Thome,' replied Carew a trifle shortly. He was beginning, dimly, to realise what fighting against the Spanish town instead of finding the mine might mean for his father. Disgrace, certainly. But what of his pardon? Would he now receive it?

Up and down, up and down walked mother and son. At last Carew drew her towards their homeward path.

'We must go in, mother. You and I must face facts now, not hide here by the quiet river. We shall have to tell our friends and relations, buy mourning clothes for ourselves and for father when he returns, and decide what to do if – if King James doesn't treat father with the respect he deserves.'

Bess, obeying the gentle pressure on her arm, turned back towards the house in Broad Street.

'The only bright spot in this day's dull weariness is that your father will be with us sooner, now that he has no further hope of gold,' Bess told Carew as they sat listlessly in the house in Broad Street, spent with sorrow.

No further hope of gold? No further hope? Carew remembered the line in his father's letter which read, 'Comfort your heart, dear Bess, I shall sorrow for us both. I shall sorrow less, because I have not long to sorrow, because not long to live.'

Was his father referring to his age? wondered Carew. Sixty-six was a good age, yet his father never seemed to realise or acknowledge that he was old. Did he suspect, then, that he would come back to England and death? Carew's loving heart thumped at the thought. His glance fell on his mother's pale, set profile. Hadn't she had enough pain in her life, he thought pitifully. Surely the King wouldn't harm his father now. So old and sad a man. Carew swallowed a lump in his throat and smiled encouragingly at Bess. She must not suspect his fears.

Carew, poor lad, was growing up fast.

When Carew was in bed, Bess had her coach brought round to the door. She went round to Marjory's lodgings, knowing her friend's husband had been attending King James at Court and hoping Marjory would be in London.

She was right. The door was opened to her knock and she was shown into the familiar sitting-room.

She told Marjory of Wat's death, dry-eyed.

'He's been dead two months, and yet it might be several years,' she told her friend. 'I've always worried about him. Getting into brawls, high-handed, high-hearted, high-mettled. I suppose in a way I've spent years waiting for news of his death, and it's made it easier for me to reconcile with reality when it came.'

'Oh my dearest, let your grief have full sway,' urged Marjory.

Bess shook her head. 'I've grieved over Wat so much these past few years, it's as though tears would be a mockery. It seems I spilled love and worry over him until with his death comes only the thought that he is at last at peace. Oh I grieve, certainly. I grieve because I'll never see him more. I'll never dandle his children on my knee and boast of my handsome eldest son. And he was young to die, Marjory. But he must have died very happy, leading his men into a fight against those vile Spaniards.'

'Will you come and stay with me? Or go down to Nicholas or Arthur?' enquired Marjory anxiously.

Bess shook her head. 'No, dearest Marjory. I shall take lodgings at Plymouth and await Sir Walter there.'

'Plymouth! Only consider, love, you know no one there,' protested Marjory.

Bess smiled. 'I shall have Carew,' she reminded her friend. 'At Plymouth I shall look over the sea, and hear the waves my love hears, and smell the salt breeze he smells. When the gulls cry overhead I shall know they will probably be the ones that will circle his masts when the *Destiny* glides into harbour. It's best, dearest of my friends, that a husband and wife should bear together the death of their son, and his death will come home to both of us strongest when the ships dock and Wat is not aboard to halloo to the waiting people.'

When Bess, Carew and all their baggage left for Plymouth, she went to Marjory's lodgings and bade her an affectionate farewell.

'You've been dearer to me than the sister I longed for as a girl,' she told Marjory. 'A better friend no man or woman has ever had. If you hear we've gone, never think we have run away. Goodbye, my dear.'

The two women clung together for a moment, then Marjory waved Bess and Carew off as they rode down the street, following the lumbering coach full of luggage.

The month Bess and Carew passed in Plymouth was one of the happiest they had spent together. The journey down was pleasant, too. They took their time, lodging at taverns or small wayside inns overnight, talking as they had never talked before.

'Would you mind very much if you had to say goodbye to England's fresh fields and mighty trees?' asked Bess as they rode through a wood which rustled with birdsong and the noises small animals make as they scuttle to hide amongst the undergrowth. The steam rising from the horses cooled under the green shade of the trees, and the flies that had been plaguing them grew less.

'England is beautiful to my eyes,' replied Carew cautiously, 'but I have never been outside this island, mother. I would be very willing to see more of the world.'

'I was brought up in the country, as was your father,' said Bess when they had passed through the wood. 'I love to hear the country sounds and smell the fresh, clean air. Of late London has seemed stifling.'

'Aye,' agreed Carew. 'I for one wouldn't care if I never saw it more.'

The answer seemed to please Bess, for she smiled tenderly at him and leaning from her horse she said, pushing back his curls from his face, 'Do you know, I've always believed folk who said you resembled me. But now you are growing to be a man you resemble your father more and more. You haven't his colouring, of course, but you have his features without a doubt.'

Carew flushed with pride, knowing his mother was presenting him with her highest accolade. Frequent glimpses of himself of late in the mirror led him to believe, too, that she was right. So many people only saw his blue eyes and light hair. They didn't notice the way adolescence was shaping his nose to the proud straightness of Sir Walter's, or how his cheekbones had interesting, adult hollows beneath them. He gave his horse a dig with his heels and it broke into a trot, then, pricked by his own excitement, began to cavort and neigh, whilst Bess laughed at them both.

They rode into Plymouth at the end of May and took their usual lodgings. The weather for once was pleasing. Cool breezes blew off the sea, but sitting on the beaches they found many a pleasant sheltered nook where Carew could lie after bathing and where Bess could find shells in the sand, strange sea-creatures in the pools, and by fixing her mind on how Walter would be taking his homeward journey, banish from her thoughts at least for the moment worry for the future.

The strange unhappy cry of the seagulls and the slap of salt water against harbour wall began to seem her life. It was as if she had never done anything else except wait here in this little town so ruled by the ocean.

She noticed a change in her friends. They treated her with unequalled kindness, as they had done before the fleet set out, but now it seemed more as though they pitied her and wanted her to be happy while she could.

Wat was dead. The fact had sunk into her brain now. But it wasn't that which made her friends eye her with such a depth of sympathy. They might not know Sir Walter as she knew him, but they must suspect, as she did, that it would need a good deal of persuasion to get him to flee the shores of England.

Lying on the quiet beach she made her

plans, every word of the speeches she must utter to get Ralegh to take the advice pressed upon her by so many of his friends.

'Don't trust the King to deal fairly, or leniently even,' they had warned Bess. 'He is still hoping that by selling Sir Walter to the Spaniards he may yet get a Spanish Princess and half a million dowry.'

Bess shook her head impatiently. Nothing could be settled until Sir Walter returned. She knew that there was a warrant out for his arrest as soon as he landed, but friends had told her there would be sufficient delay between the landing and the coming of the warrant for her to persuade him to flee the country. No one knew what the warrant would be for – Sir Walter could scarcely be arrested for failing to find a gold mine! But she didn't see how her husband's strength would stand much more imprisonment, even if it was only house arrest. She must use the time granted her to its best advantage.

Sufficient time, thought Bess wryly, with a sudden surge of honesty. Did they know what it took to persuade her husband to act against his conscience? The sands of time would run out before he would do that. No, she must plead with him for her own sake, and for Carew's. Surely then he would see that France was the better course.

Carew came bounding out of the sea and

began rubbing himself dry.

'God, mother, the water's cold despite the sunshine,' he panted. 'Come, I'll dress quickly and then let's go to the tavern at the top of the Hoe for a cup of mulled ale. I could do with something to warm me, inside and out.'

As he had promised, he dressed quickly and finally assented to being wrapped in a long cloak, though he grumbled that he felt like an old schoolmaster.

Once they had walked swiftly up the beach they entered a thick belt of trees which grew right down to the sand. This bay was only a few miles from Plymouth and one of their favourite haunts. They mounted their horses and cantered back to Plymouth, then they tethered their horses outside the tavern. Inside, the landlord saw them to a private parlour and brought them sweet hot wine, mulled ale for Carew, and a plate of oysters with brown bread and butter. He put a platter of sweetmeats and fruit tartlets down beside the oysters, and left mother and son to quench their thirst and make a hearty repast.

When at last even Carew had to admit to being comfortably warm again, and no longer as starving as a wolf, they left the tavern and stood at the top of the Hoe. Suddenly, Carew gave a scream of excitement.

'A fleet, mother, a fleet! See, already

sailing into the harbour. Let's hurry. It might well be father at last.'

They mounted their horses and urged the animals down the steep slope. Bess, eyeing the ships, thought they looked remarkably like the battered remains of a fleet that had been almost a year at sea.

'Can you see the name of the flagship from here, Carew?' asked Bess breathlessly. 'The wind of our going has blurred my eyesight for a moment.'

Carew strained his eyes and again shouted unnaturally loudly, 'Yes, mother. It's the *Destiny*, the *Destiny* at last. Father's come back to us alright, I can see him on the deck. Oh, hooray, hooray! See him? He's managed to pick us out, he's waving!'

The ships drew alongside the quay and Ralegh was first down the gangplank. He was burned brown as a nut, but his hollow eyes bespoke suffering and sleepless nights and his hair was completely white.

He clapsed Bess fiercely in his arms, muttering, 'My darling, my only love,' whilst Carew chatted to some of the sailors as they stood swaying on the quay, their feet betraying them once the deck no longer heaved beneath them.

'Some of the fleet turned pirate,' a sailor was telling Carew. 'Two more craft we left in Ireland. Your father was begged to remain there by the Earl of Cork – a fine gentleman he is, the Earl – but he insisted that he had given his word to return to England.'

Ralegh turned, one arm still around Bess's shoulders, and said, 'Carew, my son! How you've grown in my absence! I would scarcely have known you.' He threw his free arm round Carew's strong young back and walked uncertainly between them up from the harbour towards their lodgings.

The wanderer, so long awaited, had returned at last.

FIFTEEN

BROKEN PROMISES

That evening in their lodgings, Bess let Sir Walter talk. She knew he must be longing to explain more fully what had happened on the ill-fated voyage; how Wat had died; where he was buried. She had braced herself to hear these things, and hear them she did. Keymis had buried Wat before the high altar in the church at San Thome.

She was glad that she had done with sorrowing for Wat, for now she was able to comfort Ralegh, who gave way to a passion of remorse.

'If only I had overruled them all and led the expedition myself, then Wat would never have charged straight on to an army at the head of a few pikemen,' he cried.

Bess was firm. 'You mustn't blame yourself, dear heart, nor Keymis. No more self-reproach for what cannot be altered. Promise me?'

Sir Walter, leaning his white head against

her smooth shoulder, promised.

That night, Bess let him talk himself into some sort of peace. She knew he must sleep. Then tomorrow he would be in a better state to hear her proposals that they should fly to France whilst there was yet time.

He had arrived home on the 21st June, 1618. The following day Bess began pleading with Sir Walter to take Carew and herself aboard the *Destiny* and sail.

'Oh, you of little faith,' teased her husband. 'Surely the worst the King can do is refuse me entry to Court once more? Then we shall rusticate together, Bess, watching the roses grow. The King has done me ill enough; surely now my shame and sorrows are sufficient, without him adding to them by imprisonment and disgrace?'

'My love,' urged Bess, 'there is a warrant out for your arrest. Great men, friends also, have urged me to persuade you to flee the country. You have returned as you promised. We can stay in Plymouth awhile and then take ship for France.'

'The King didn't mean that, when he took my promise to return,' growled Ralegh.

'No, he meant to please Spain. I'm sure, if we could see into his devious mind, that he wishes you would go to France and clear his conscience! You're a thorn in his flesh, a constant reminder of his own weakness.'

'My bird, I'd please you if I could,'

answered Ralegh at last. 'But I'm an old man, sore at heart over the death of my son, sick at heart over the death of my hopes. All I have left is my honour. Don't take that away from me. Anyway, what use would I be to the King of France now? Sick, old, ague-ridden. I must go to London and face whatever fate awaits me there, but surely it won't be so fearsome?'

However, in his weakened state he dallied at Plymouth, where the citizens treated him with love and respect and he had the quietness he longed for.

Carew refused to join his mother's pleading that they should flee to France.

'I'm proud of father,' he told Bess fiercely. 'Would you have me persuade him to flee, against his conscience and inclinations?'

'I believe France is life. London, death,' Bess stated boldly.

She saw Carew's face pucker, but he didn't cry. 'Father would say "rather an honourable death than dishonourable flight",' he reminded her, and she realised he shared her fears, but could not help her against his own conscience.

A lethargy settled on Bess when she realised Sir Walter wouldn't be persuaded. When he told her at the end of a fortnight to pack her baggage, for they would leave for London in the morning, she did as she was bidden. No reproaches came from her lips and Myers, helping her to pack, thought the world undervalued Lady Ralegh.

It's a difficult thing, thought Myers, to go towards a King's anger. But it's more difficult to put a cheerful face over grave thoughts, pretending to one you love so dearly that all would be well, as her mistress did.

They set off on a hot morning in early July. The coach was overfull with all their luggage, but all the Raleghs preferred to ride in the open air.

'Am I tired by the heat?' Sir Walter said, laughing. 'Why, my bird, compared with the heat of Guiana, this is a gentle spring warmth caressing my old bones.'

They rode slowly through town and countryside. Sir Walter drank in the scents and sounds around them. The green bracken brushed the bellies of their horses. Its warm, heady scent seemed the embodiment of all things English to Ralegh.

But the journey wasn't half done before they met Sir Lewis Stukeley, a kinsman of Ralegh's, coming to meet them with orders for his arrest. Sir Walter had done many kindnesses for his young cousin Lewis, and was glad to have so pleasant a jailer, especially when Stukeley advised him to return to Plymouth and sell the remaining tobacco aboard the *Destiny* so that he would have money by him.

After the sale, Stukeley agreed, after some polite hesitation, to take a portion of the money for himself, since without his forethought the sale wouldn't have been made.

'We'll divide it up in happier times,' he told Ralegh. 'Now we'd better make for London speedily – returning to Plymouth has delayed us a great deal.'

He showed Ralegh a letter which had arrived from the King, with a formal and urgent warrant for Sir Walter's arrest.

'Think you this means another trial?' asked Ralegh doubtfully, but Stukeley could only shrug uneasily.

'Who knows the King's mind?' he asked. 'Certainly not I. Maybe not the King himself at this juncture.'

So in order to gain time to write his defence, Ralegh feigned sickness. He refused food and acted as one mad. They were at a tavern in Salisbury at the time and each night Bess smuggled food to her husband from the 'White Hart', which he ate ravenously whilst scarcely stopping the urgent task of writing down his case to prove to the King that he was no traitor guilty of treason but a man of goodwill who had done his best and, failing, had come back to face his King.

When his defence was written he 'recovered' and the journey was continued. But when they arrived in London, Ralegh was refused an audience with King James.

Back once more in Broad Street, under house arrest, many urged him openly to fly the country and Ralegh was made to see it was his only hope of life. The French Ambassador urged it too, not only because his country wanted Ralegh as admiral, but because no Frenchman wanted to see the heir to the English throne marry a Spaniard. A French Princess could be found for Charles, forming an English–French alliance.

When the King sent messages saying he wouldn't see Ralegh, Sir Walter and Bess had a long discussion in the safety of their bed.

'You were right, Bess. I shouldn't have put any faith in James,' admitted Ralegh gloomily. 'Think you the French are right also? That I can best help my country by escaping to France so that the Spanish marriage will come to nought?'

Bess said thankfully, 'Oh, my dear love, if only it's not too late! Carew and I will follow you as soon as we may. Will you really leave?'

'I'll really try,' said Sir Walter gravely. 'For your sakes I'll make the attempt. Now sleep, darling, your worries are over.'

It took several days to arrange an escape. Sir Lewis Stukeley came forward with the offer of a boat to escape down the Thames to where the ships lay at anchor, and vowed he would serve James no more but would go to France with Ralegh.

Bess and Walter were touched by such devotion. Lewis was the nephew of that Sir Richard Grenville who had died aboard the *Revenge*, a man revered by Sir Walter from his earliest years. Now, he said, Lewis showed his likeness to his noble uncle.

At last the little boat left the quayside near Broad Street at dead of night. Bess and Carew, muffled in dark cloaks, waved a quiet farewell and returned home – to wait once more, feeling quite lightheaded with relief.

Meanwhile, Ralegh sat in the boat, hearing the sounds of water lapping against the prow and the sleepy chirping of waterbirds disturbed by their passing. He was watching the dim shapes of houses on the bank when he thought he saw something through the thick darkness. He drew Stukeley's attention to the shape behind them.

'Lewis, is that another craft? My eyesight's not what it was,' he said anxiously, grasping his cousin's arm in his quick, nervous way.

'Yes, it's probably some nobleman going home after an assignation,' suggested his cousin. 'Don't worry, Sir Walter, there's nothing to harm us there.'

Ralegh leaned back and tried to relax. There was no moon and the sky was pin-pricked with stars. How small they seemed, thought Ralegh, after the flaunting brilliance of the stars over Guiana. How small and bright and dear!

The smell of waterweed and the rocking motion of the boat had almost lulled him to sleep by the time they reached Greenwich. It was then that the other craft drew noiselessly but steadily closer.

'What do they want?' he muttered uneasily to Stukeley.

'Why nothing. Others are abroad on the river at night, cousin. You must surely have been so yourself,' answered Stukeley soothingly. 'You have been in ill health, for it was never your way to start at shadows. See, I fear them not.'

The other boat, larger and full of men, crept alongside and as the two boats bumped gently, Ralegh handed some of his precious possessions to Stukeley, bidding him in an urgent undertone to 'Take these to Bess, my friend.'

'I will certainly do so,' muttered Stukeley softly, and then aloud, 'And now I arrest you in the King's name,' he went on as men began to swarm aboard.

For one long moment piercing black eyes looked into shifty grey ones. Then, 'Sir Lewis,' Ralegh said quietly, 'that was not well done. These actions will not turn out to your credit.'

What a mild reproof for the man soon to be known as 'Sir Judas Stukeley'! But Stukeley knew nothing of what was to come. He took Sir Walter to the Tower, eagerly snatching at his cousin's personal belongings.

He'd done pretty well, Stukeley thought complaisantly. Nearly £1,000 expenses for bringing Sir Walter back from Plymouth. All the money and jewels found on Sir Walter's person, and the tobacco money from the *Destiny*. Now he could collect his blood money from the King and he would have done handsomely out of the affair.

All this while, in the house in Broad Street, Bess and Carew slept peacefully, convinced that after so many years of imprisonment Ralegh was on his way to freedom.

By the following morning all London knew that Ralegh was in the Tower. By the day after all London knew he had been betrayed, that his flight had been forced on him by treachery so that James could say he was 'caught whilst attempting to escape'.

Bess wept bitterly. She could have saved him this. She knew it was her own urgent pleas that had made him resolve on a fresh start abroad, for her sake and Carew's. Now she too had betrayed him, albeit unknowingly.

She heard with dismay that he was to die

on the charge of treason for which he'd been condemned fifteen years ago. He would have no other hearing.

Thus no one would hear his defence, nor have to find an answer to the fact that if he was guilty of treason James wouldn't have sent him to Guiana.

'You have lived like a star, at which the world has gazed. And like a star you must fall, when the firmament is shaked,' pronounced Sir Francis Bacon. Ralegh heard the meaningless words in a daze, whilst his mind went back to the day Bacon had told him, 'Your commission as Admiral is as good as a pardon, I'll stake my life.'

But it was Ralegh's life that had been staked, and he had lost.

Bess steeled herself for one desperate last appeal to the King. Carew wrote to James, pleading for his father's life to be spared. Bess would have knelt to the King, but she knew by now it would only annoy him. So she went to Queen Anne, who had ever been their friend. The Queen wrote to George Villiers, Duke of Buckingham, whom she found a refreshing change after the obnoxious self-opinionated Carr.

In his turn, the Duke of Buckingham tried to intercede for Ralegh, but King James fled from his friends as though they were foes. He wanted only one thing. To be rid – rid – rid of the man who took his friends and had stolen the love of the dead prince. This time, Ralegh must die.

In his haste and anger he couldn't sign the death warrant fast enough. So he fixed the execution for 19th November. It was the day of the Lord Mayor's Show, and James hoped the people who had flocked to London to look their last on Ralegh might be kept away from the execution by the show.

Bess had one only of her many requests granted. She was allowed to live with her husband in the Tower until a few days before his execution. Then she made her way back to Broad Street, where Carew and Myers awaited her.

Ralegh spent his last night at the old Gate House of Westminster. Many friends visited him and found him smoking, jesting and almost, it seemed, happy.

'Why, Jack, not many men have two last nights on earth as I have done,' he replied to a friend who censured his lack of gravity. 'Now there are no more worries or sadness. Soon I shall be truly free, beyond the reach of that little man at last.'

His friends gazed at him with awe. What a man, who could dismiss his persecutor lightly with the words 'little man', who could look forward to death as an end to tedious earthly worries and a beginning of true freedom!

But when Bess was allowed to see him, there were no jests. He had told his valet to trim his beard and hair, and stood up to greet her, a tall straight-backed man, whose sloe-black eyes were weary but still bright.

Bess thought of all the things she wanted to say. But all she knew was that she had always loved him, and though her love would never perish, he must. She began to speak but her voice was suspended by tears as she flung herself, weeping, into those beloved arms for the last time.

At last she managed to control her tears, drying her eyes on Sir Walter's handkerchief. She whispered brokenly that the Lords of the Council had granted her the disposal of his body, the most charity she could wring from them.

Stroking her dishevelled hair back from her broad, peaceful brow, Sir Walter said gently, 'It is well, my bird, that you should have the disposal of that, dead, which living was so often denied you.'

The unfaded blue eyes gazed through tear-swollen lids into his. 'When you die, something in me will die. You've been my life, Walter. No one but you has meaning. Everyone will seem a ghost beside your vigorous memory. Already you've faced tomorrow.'

'Yes. Tomorrow will end the frettings, the worries, the ambitions which have delighted and tormented me for so many years. But for you, dear Bess, all this must go on. We must talk not of endings but of beginnings. I'd like you to re-marry.'

Bess shook her head, her soft lips forming a firm line.

'I'm fifty-three, old enough in all faith to take care of myself and our son. For myself, I would wish to see Carew a man. Then my one desire will be to join you.'

He would have scolded her for obstinacy, but this was not the moment for scoldings. It was his last chance to show Bess how truly he had loved her. Through the long absences, whilst he was paying court to Elizabeth, during the long sojourn in the Tower. Their love had been a perfect thing, neither must mar their last moments.

So they talked of the past, and Bess spoke the name that had been unmentioned between them for twenty-six years.

'I loved Damerei. I often feel it was our fault that he died. But now, I'm sure it was for the best. Who knows what happens to the souls of tiny babies? Maybe Damerei knew best when he left this life before tasting the sweets and bitters.'

'So long you've carried Damerei's memory in your heart and never forgotten him,' marvelled Ralegh. 'I forgot him because it was politic to do so. It was a cruelty to forbid discussion of the child even between ourselves, my bird. I'm sorry.'

Bess, cradled in his arms, said gently, 'Never mind, sweetheart. Never mind. No other harm did you do me either by thought, word or deed. My life has been enriched beyond my wildest dreams by your love. But I must leave at midnight – we have only a minute. Goodbye, my only love.'

'Goodbye, my bird. Don't sorrow for me. I'm an old man, going to a mercifully quick death.'

There was a knock and the keeper put his head round the door and beckoned to Bess. She tightened her hold on Sir Walter for one breathless moment, then turned and walked steadily towards the door. Only when she reached the top of the stairs did she turn for one last glimpse of the man she had lived for and would have died for.

Ralegh's face was calm, but he said softly, 'Remember me, my bird.'

Bess nodded speechlessly and ran down to her waiting carriage. The words from one of the many plays she had seen were running through her head. 'Pray love, remember.' She didn't know where she'd heard them, or when. Her mind fretted over the little sentence until it grew more complete in her mind.

'There's rosemary, that's for remembrance; pray love, remember.'

It was running through her mind as she lay

in her bed and something prompted her to climb out and go over to the bunches of dried sweet herbs she kept to go in her posies. She chose a sprig of rosemary and climbed back into bed with it, holding it against her bare breasts, letting the tears roll down and salt the brittle leaves.

Ralegh, alone now in his little room, sat down at the table to write. He wrote his will, giving great thought to the phrasing so that there should be no slip, as there had been over Sherborne.

He wrote out nine succinct denials of the charges against him. He even found time, before his eyes closed in the sleep that would bring him clear-eyed and unfuddled to his ordeal, to write out a poem on the flyleaf of his Bible.

Even such is Time! who takes in trust
Our youth, our joys and all we have,
And pays us but with earth and dust;
Who in the dark and silent grave,
When we have wandered all our ways,
Shuts up the story of our days.
But from that earth, that grave, that dust,
The Lord shall raise me up, I trust.

Then and only then did he go to his bed, preparing himself by such action so that he should appear at his best on the morrow.

SIXTEEN

THE SHARP MEDICINE

Whilst Ralegh slept, Bess could not. She paced the floor of her room. Now and again Myers scuttled in and made up the fire so that her mistress should not feel the cold. Bess found her mind going over the details. She had arranged for her coach to be present at her husband's execution so that the head might be put in the red leather bag she had given the coachman and taken to the embalmer's.

During the long night she made up her mind she would never look inside that bag. Never try to see those beloved features unnatural in death. But she would keep it by her side until she died, in remembrance of him. She thought of other things. She had sent his best clothes to the old Gate House, for that was how he would want the people to remember him.

He was still in mourning for Wat, so it was a sober outfit. Sober, but rich. She had

276

packed his tawny satin doublet and black taffeta breeches, his ash-coloured silk stockings and black velvet shoes. For warmth, so that he might not tremble with ague which might be mistaken for fear, he had asked for his long gown of black wrought velvet and a laced skullcap to wear under his hat.

Never had a night seemed so long to Bess. Yet when the first pale streaks of dawn appeared in the sky she trembled and turned pale. The day of Sir Walter's death had dawned.

Desperately, she sat close to the fire and drove her mind back into the past. She remembered the day she and Ralegh had first spoken to each other. At Greenwich Palace, in the room used as the Queen's wardrobe. She remembered the sunshine flooding into the room, his smiling, sarcastic look, the swift, firm stride with which he passed amongst the maids of honour. She remembered his audacious teasing of Queen Elizabeth. She remembered, too, how he had loved his Queen. Pictures of their early married life, the baby Wat in his swaddling clothes held in his father's arms, then running about in petticoats, then being breeched, ran through her head.

She thought of the many times she had waved Ralegh goodbye. As he went off to Elizabeth's Court, Ireland, Jersey, and the voyage to Guiana. She remembered the tensions and the fun of life under Elizabeth. Then her mind shuddered away from those years in the Tower. Perhaps it was for the best that he should die the quick death of the axe, and not moulder in the Tower until the straw death overtook him there.

As the morning brightened she still sat in her bedchamber, huddled beside the fire. Presently Carew and Myers joined her there. The three of them sat, silent now, living in their minds the scene in the Palace Yard.

Ralegh awoke from an uneasy sleep, glad that at length day had dawned and the last act would soon be over. He almost laughed at himself as he ate a hearty breakfast and smoked a last pipe of tobacco. But many friends would be present round the scaffold and he knew he must go into the cold, crisp morning with a full stomach and a quiet mind so that he was at his best and would make a good end. I'll die in such a way that I'll be remembered for it, he thought, sucking at his pipe and thinking how annoyed James would be when he heard his hated prisoner had enjoyed a smoke before his execution. James, the wine bibber, didn't approve of smoking. But then, he didn't approve of anything Ralegh did.

He walked slowly and a little stiffly into the Palace Yard, having to squeeze his way through the press and throng of people. Thinking of the show that was supposed to keep the Palace Yard empty, he thought wryly how the Lord Mayor must be cursing him. But he could comfort himself with the thought that after the execution the people could then go on to enjoy the show.

He raised his eyes to the balconies and windows round the yard. They were crowded with many friends, and he thanked God in his mind that he was to die within the sight of so many pairs of eyes, noble and simple, who would take a report of his last words and spread them so that even the Court and most especially his dear Bess would hear how he made his confession and died well.

Because his voice was weak from his many months at sea and in prison, the lords and nobles came out from their places and crowded round him on the scaffold, whilst he told everyone what he had tried in vain to tell the King – that the voyage to Guiana had been carried out in accordance with the King's own wishes.

He spoke also of Essex's death, which he had missed because he thought Essex would rather he was not present. His sadness when he spoke of Essex wanting a reconciliation with him after he had left the scaffold was the only time his voice shook slightly.

Then he was done. He stood before them,

a straight old man, with the look of piercing intelligence still in his black eyes, but those same eyes were already taking on a look of peace. He refused to discuss James' conduct, for, he said, 'What have I to do with kings, who am about to go before the King of Kings?'

The Sheriffs cleared the scaffold, and Ralegh removed his long gown and doublet. He gave his hat and some money to attendants and stood in the nipping morning air, a once proud man, who had humbled his pride before the crowd when he made his confession. Yet even half clothed, white-haired and about to die, there was not a soul in the crowd who was not aware that he looked upon a great man.

Ralegh asked to feel the axe, to see that it was sharp. Feeling the edge, he remarked with a touch of his old wry humour, 'A sharp medicine, but it is a physician for all diseases.'

He refused to be blindfolded, saying mockingly, 'Think you I fear the shadow of the axe when I fear not the axe itself?'

He lay his head upon the block and told the headsman to strike when he signalled with his hand. For a moment he prayed quietly, then gave the signal. The man, trembling like a startled hare, found his arms were like wool and he couldn't lift the axe.

Ralegh glanced up at him impatiently and said rallyingly, 'What do'st fear? Strike, man. Strike!'

Twice the axe rose and fell before Ralegh's head was severed from his body. As the headsman held up the head, wordlessly and still trembling, a voice rang out from the crowd.

'We have not such another head to be cut off.'

The rumble of the wheels of her coach brought Bess back into the world of reality. She glanced at Carew and saw by his whitened face that he realised the significance. Without a word the three of them fell to their knees, the boy and Myers crying softly. Bess felt she was crying inwardly – no, bleeding inwardly.

The impossible had happened. Her husband was dead and without him life would have little meaning. Yet she remembered the words he had spoken the night before. She mustn't grieve so much that she made herself ill and unable to take care of their son. Now he was all that she had left.

She touched Carew's arm. 'My love, I must take my bath now, and then dress. Do you go and bath also. You are young and must weep. I am not young, and have done with weeping. Go, Carew, I'll see you presently.'

When Carew had left, Bess wrapped her long bedgown about her and said abruptly, 'Whilst the menservants fill my bath, Myers, would you bring me pen and paper? I must write to my brother Nicholas.'

Two menservants came in with big jugs of steaming water whilst Myers fetched the pen and paper. Bess balanced the ink on her dressing table and started to write.

She began the letter to Nicholas quite calmly, begging him that he would allow her to bury Ralegh's body in his church at Beddington. But by the end of the letter the long pent-up turmoil was beginning to break through. She knew her hand was shaking and saw the paper through a blur of tears.

'The lords have given me his dead body,' she wrote in letters and spelling so wild that Nicholas had difficulty in deciphering it, 'though they denied me his life. God hold me in my wits.'

As she finished she could feel how easy it would be to plunge into the pit of madness. But she had to think of young Carew. He was fourteen, just at the age when he would need her most. And with the King's displeasure hanging over all who bore the name of Ralegh, she could not let him down.

She sanded the letter and handed it to Myers. As she stood up, from her gown there dropped a crushed sprig of rosemary.

She remembered the long, dreadful night and her strange recollection of that fragment of – ah, she had it, a play! A young girl had spoken the lines, she recalled the scene. The girl all in white, her hands full of flowers, speaking a line with each blossom as she cast it into a grave.

'There's rosemary; that's for remembrance; pray love, remember,' she murmured. The lines held comfort for her, though she needed no rosemary now to aid her memory.

The bath was ready, steaming in front of the fire, and Myers stood by it ready to lend her a hand in and out of the water. In the relaxing warmth, Bess felt a pang of shame that she could enjoy the scented soap as she rubbed it over her skin, the warm clothes she presently allowed Myers to put on her dried, quiescent body.

She looked at her thick plaits of hair hanging down to her knees. The once burnished gold showed a lot of white now. In death was her salvation, but she must first see Carew firmly established in his career. Sir Walter had wished it.

Myers did her hair and presently she went rather shakily downstairs. Carew supported his mother, realising for the first time that she was looking her age.

When they had breakfasted, they sat and

looked at each other across the table.

'We must now make ourselves a nuisance to James, otherwise we shall starve,' announced Bess with a certain amount of satisfaction.

For years she and Carew made themselves a nuisance to King James. Ralegh himself, by his speech before his death, had made James a person to be avoided, not to be trusted. Ralegh's writings continued to be widely read and praised by all except the King.

Bess and Carew kept on the house in Broad Street and hired a house in the country, too. But Carew grew up and lived out his life in the shadow of a great man.

He went to Oxford, as his brother and father had done before him, and after Oxford went to Court. But he didn't stay there long. The King, catching sight of him, so like his father except for his fair colouring, cried out, 'Take him away. It's like seeing Ralegh's ghost.'

Carew's own particular fight was the fight to regain Sherborne, something he knew his father would have applauded. He was never successful. Bess fought, too, to retain papers, maps and globes, books even, belonging to her husband. To her they were of great sentimental value but they were not of much actual worth. The King seized all he could simply because she was the wife of the man he had become to believe his arch-enemy, even in death.

But as though to prove the superiority of the Raleghs, Bess outlived James, and most of her own generation. Her house on Broad Street was burned down, she suffered various misfortunes, but none as great as that of long life.

For hers was a long life indeed. She dragged through the weary days, drained of colour now that her lover wasn't with her, but she never ceased to fight to clear Ralegh's name until merciful death overtook her, in 1647, when she was eighty-two and had outlived Sir Walter by twenty-nine years.

Carew, looking at her on her death bed, thought how brave and passionate and colourful had been this lady's life – this beautiful lady, for even at eighty-two nothing could take away the beautiful bone structure of her face, the never-fading blue of her eyes, and the wavy thickness of her long white hair.

But as he bent over the bed to hear her faint whisper, he felt he understood completely how she was feeling.

'At last, my love,' she said tenderly. 'Oh, at long, long last.'

1	21	41	61	(81)	101	121	141	161	181
2	22	42	62	82	102	122	142	162	182
3	23	43	63	83	103	123	143	163	183
4	24	44	64	84	104	124	144	164	(184)
5	25	45	65	85	105	125	145	165	185
6	26	46	66	86	106	126	146	166	186
7	27	47	67	87	107	127	147	167	187
8	28	48	68	88	108	128	148	168	188
9	29	49	69	89	109	129	149	169	189
10	30	50	70	90	110	130	150	170	190
11	31	51	71	91	111	131	151	171	191
12	32	52	72	92	112	132	152	172	192
13	33	53	73	93	113	133	153	173	193
14	34	54	74	94	114	134	154	174	194
(15)	35	55	75	95	115	135	155	175	195
16	36	56	76	96	116	136	156	176	196
17	37	57	77	97	117	137	157	177	197
18	38	58	78	98	118	138	158	178	198
19	39	59	79	99	119	139	159	179	199
20	40	60	80	100	120	140	160	180	200

201	211	221	231	241	251	261	271	281	291
202	212	222	232	242	252	262	272	282	292
203	213	223	233	243	253	263	273	283	293
204	214	224	234	244	254	264	274	284	294
205	215	225	235	245	255	265	275	285	295
206	216	226	236	246	256	266	276	286	296
207	217	227	237	247	257	267	277	287	297
208	218	228	238	248	258	268	278	288	298
209	219	229	239	249	259	269	279	289	299
210	220	230	240	250	260	270	280	290	300

301	310	319	328	337	346
302	311	320	329	338	347
303	312	321	330	(339)	348
304	313	322	331	340	349
305	314	323	332	341	350
306	315	324	333	342	
307	316	325	334	343	
308	317	326	335	344	
309	318	327	336	345	